CHURCH END

BY

COLIN BRODERICK

Copyright © 2020 by Colin Broderick

All rights reserved. No part of the book may be reproduced in any form or by any electronic or mechanical means, including information storage and retrieval systems, without permission in writing from the publisher, except by a reviewer who may quote brief passages in a review.

The characters and events in this book are fictitious. Any similarity to real persons, living or dead, is coincidental and not intended by the author.

Cover design by Daria Milas

ISBN-13: 9798680676639

*This book is dedicated to Rachel. My everything. My always.
And to our children: Erica, Samuel, and Bruce.*

Prologue

In writing this prologue I have tried to think about what information is needed to understand the novel itself. Perhaps none is needed. Perhaps it's possible to read the novel as is. The word "prologue" seems to incite a sense of tediousness with readers. But, God help me, and you, I have decided that this particular novel deserves an introduction of sorts. So here it is.

(Feel free to skip a couple of pages here and just begin the book. I won't judge you.)

Church End was the first full book I ever wrote. I wrote it in a frenzy when I was living in Riverdale in the Bronx, when I was twenty-six years old. I had no plans for the book. I wanted to write a novel. I had a rough premise in my head. I started writing, and as the characters appeared, I simply followed them wherever they went. In that regard it is the most innocent, the most pure, of all my books. The ending was as much a surprise to me as it will be to the reader.

It was a wonderful adventure to write this book. I wrote the first draft in just six weeks. Ah, youth.

I printed a few copies of the manuscript. Had them bound at a local printing shop and gave them to a few friends and family and moved on with my life. In early 2020 right at the beginning of the pandemic, we had just moved. I was sorting through old boxes and came across an old faded copy of the manuscript. Since this was the only version I had, I decided that I better make some effort to type it up so that I would have a copy in case I lost or damaged the original.

As I began to type I started recording readings of each chapter which I posted to YouTube. People seemed to be enjoying the book. An audience was assembling. I decided that I would commit to it, give it a polish, and self-publish it for posterity.

Twenty-six years after I wrote the initial draft, I feel it necessary to clarify some of the historical issues at hand. It's important that I clarify the time period, and the political turmoil of the day so that you, the reader, might better understand the essence of the murderous rage at the heart of the novel's protagonist.

Perhaps I am already anticipating the chorus of criticism at writing a novel that speaks to the rage I felt as a young Irish man toward the English.

Let me start by saying, I no longer feel that rage. But I do feel it's important to acknowledge that at one time the rage existed, and the rage is a historical fact of my life that I refuse to whitewash. It's important to talk about our history in honest terms. Catholics in Ireland have been guilted for decades into silence over some of our most painful and transformative historical moments:

The 1916 Easter Rising.

The Famine.

Bloody Sunday.

Best not to talk too much of such things lest we upset our English neighbors to the east.

Well, to hell with that, I say. The only way to ensure our Irish history is not robbed from us entirely is to pass on some semblance of the emotional truth to the generations in our wake who have been raised on an educational curriculum that seems like it might well have been blessed by the Queen herself.

To the novel at hand:

In 1986, when I was eighteen years old, I left my home in County Tyrone, Northern Ireland, to go to work construction in London. The North of Ireland, the six counties, at that time were going through some of the harshest years of a sectarian war known as The Troubles. Work opportunities for a young Catholic lad consisted primarily of two key choices: farming or construction. It was painful, to say the least, to watch our Protestant counterparts, young Protestant lads like ourselves, walk away with all the cushy jobs, the nice houses, and the fancy college education.

The overwhelming majority of Catholics at that time finished school at sixteen and immediately entered the workforce. Many of us emigrated to London or New York where the real money was to be made working construction. Moving away was also a form of escape. The Troubles were raging, young men were being murdered. Northern Ireland was a war zone.

So what were The Troubles? It sounds so unassuming... like something you might say if your car battery died, or a guitar string snapped.

For those of you unfamiliar with that particular time period in Ireland, I'll try to break it down for you in simplistic terms:

Ireland is made up of thirty-two counties. The Northern six counties were (and still are) occupied by the British. Britain had occupied all of Ireland once upon a time but after the war of independence the southern twenty-six counties established what is known as the Irish Free State in 1922.

Meanwhile, the British established a hard border across the northeast part of the country, lopping off six counties they decided to keep for themselves. Irish nationalist Catholics in that part of the country were extremely upset that they were now being forced to live under the rule of a British flag and pay tax to a monarchy they despised.

Northern Irish Protestants who were faithful to the British flag, and the monarchy, were rewarded with all the good jobs in the country, and the best housing. They controlled the police force and the legal system.

Catholics were subjugated and persecuted at every turn. We faced humiliation at British checkpoints practically every time we left our homes. Snotty young British soldiers demanding to know where we were coming from, where we were going to, and why.

We had become a nuisance in our own country.

In the late sixties Catholics banded together to take to the streets to demand equality.

CHURCH END

What began in 1968 as a civil rights movement by Catholics in Northern Ireland pushing for basic equality in housing, education, and government-allocated jobs, quickly devolved into a full-blown sectarian war after the British Armed Forces opened fire on peaceful civil rights marchers in Derry on Sunday, January 30, 1972. Fourteen innocent Catholics were slaughtered that day... many of them were children.

The Troubles had begun.

On one side you had Irish Catholics, represented militarily by the IRA (the Irish Republican Army) and on the other, the British Nationalists, Protestants in Northern Ireland, represented primarily by the British Army.

By 1986, the period of this particular novel, tensions between Ireland and England, (Catholics and Protestants) were at an all-time high. Shootings and car bombs, and random military checkpoints were an everyday part of life.

The life of a young Catholic man felt doubly oppressive because in the eyes of the British, every young Catholic boy in Northern Ireland was a potential terrorist.

It was a crippling burden to bear. So when I left Northern Ireland for London at eighteen, I wasn't so much emigrating for work as I was fleeing a cauldron of stifling political tension for a life where a young man might get drunk and stoned and listen to Pink Floyd with some sense of freedom and abandon.

Of course, life in London as a young Irish man came with its own sense of social oppression. In the eyes of many English we were still a bunch of murdering terrorists. What the average English person knew of young Irish men they were seeing on the telly on the six o'clock news. And believe me, the English media did not shed a very favorable light on our plight.

I arrived in London and fell in right away with a crew of Northern Irish ex-pats squatting on a government owned housing estate in Harlesden. The housing estate was called Church End.

Church End was a sprawling housing development that ran the length of Church Road in Harlesden, bracketed on one end by the police station, on the other by The White Horse Tavern.

Over the next two years tensions increased in Northern Ireland and I bounced back and forth between Church End Estate and my home in County Tyrone.

It was a particularly volatile moment in Northern Ireland. Young Irish boys were being slaughtered in the streets under Margaret Thatcher's Shoot to Kill Policy.

Thatcher had decided to forgo all legal pretense in dealing with the situation in Northern Ireland. If a young Irish lad was becoming too much of a threat, then the British Army simply shot him. No trial. No jail. No justice.

More than anything else the murderous rage at the heart of the novel's protagonist is born out of that period of Margaret Thatcher's Shoot to Kill policy. I attended open coffin wakes of friends, eighteen-year-old boys who'd been shot in the face at point blank by the British Army's Special Air Service, the SAS as they were known. Young Catholic boys who could have just as easily been arrested and jailed were being slaughtered in the streets like dogs.

After twenty-six years it was time to take the novel out of the box. Time to acknowledge the rage. Acknowledge the trauma. Honor those who died, by continuing to tell our side of the story.

This is a work of fiction.

It's a telling of the emotional imprint of my childhood.

I have built a career out of telling my story.

Church End is part of that story.

London 1986

Chapter 1

"You lazy shower of wankers better get your fingers out of yer holes and get these fucken doors hung by lunchtime or you can pack your shit and get the fuck off my site." That was Harry, the English ganger. He stopped in front of Nial and barked again, "You hear me, Paddy?"

The last thing Nial needed right now was the sound of an Englishman yelling at him. It wasn't yet ten o'clock and Nial was exhausted already. He'd been up most of the night, sitting by the bedroom window, watching the lights of the cars going by on Church Road. He'd had the nightmare again, the same dream that had taken him from his sleep for months. He was at home, back in Tyrone, sitting on the front step of his parent's house. The afternoon light cutting through the old ash tree throwing shadows on the damp lawn. His older brother, Cathal, was running toward him, yelling his name… "Nial. Nial." The soldier raised his gun and fired. One shot. Cathal's face turned to blood.

"Are you deaf, Paddy!" Harry yelled. Nial tightened his grip on the shaft of the hammer that dangled in his right hand.

A carpenter working next to Nial dropped his tools where he stood and, without even a glance at Harry, walked straight out the door past him, making a bee line for the canteen across the muddy yard. Harry spun around and yelled after him.

"Where the fuck do you think you're going?"

"For me fucken tae," Seamus growled, without turning around. It was breakfast time. Harry gritted his teeth and stormed off as the rest of the men followed suit. He wasn't going to stand between a bunch of hungry Irishmen and their morning tea. Nobody in their right mind would start that war.

Barkley, one of the Jamaican brickies, strolled by and gave Nial a nod, and a wink so imperceptible it could have been mistaken for an eye twitch. He was on his way to smoke a spliff out on the roof and he knew Nial liked to tag along. It was a daily ritual among a handful of the workers: ditch breakfast for a good old-fashioned smoke. Just enough to soften the corners of the day. Nial caught John The Burner give him a disappointing glance. The nod-and-a-wink hadn't been discreet enough to elude his one eagle eye. The Burner was an older Irish carpenter who'd taken Nial under his wing on the site. He wore a black eye patch over one eye. And yes, Nial had asked him the big question: "What happened your eye?"

"What eye?" The Burner had replied, and Nial had

dropped it. No one knew the story of the eye patch. But everyone knew the one eye he had was enough. The Burner missed nothing.

Nial was only eighteen when he got the start here a few months back, and The Burner had covered for him until he got his feet under him. Showed him how to use a tape measure, how to swing a hammer, and how to use a handsaw without cutting the hands off himself. The Burner was old school. A drinking man. The Burner had no time for druggies. Joints were for druggies.

Barkley sensing Nial was not behind him had turned and caught The Burner's disappointing glance also. He stopped in the doorway and called to the older Irishman. "Come on up and smoke the Ganga, Johnnyman, put a smile on that sad Irish face of yours." The Burner responded by gently rubbing his thumb over the razor-sharp wood chisel he held in his right hand. Barkley chuckled and sauntered off muttering something about Paddy drinking too much, gonna die young.

Nial decided to forgo the smoke for the day. He threw off his tool belt and followed the others across the mucky yard to the canteen.

The canteen was a makeshift plywood structure. A room large enough to seat about eighty hungry Micks shoulder to shoulder at rough plywood tables.

Inside, the place smelled like greasy bacon, wet boots, and cigarette smoke. The lads formed a shuffling line down one side of the room toward the food. They were a groggy, unkempt bunch. There wasn't a head in the room that had seen a comb in weeks. They lived alone, these men, in tiny bedsits and squats, mostly in the north of the city around Harlesden, Wilsden, and Cricklewood, like Nial did. There would be nobody waiting for them when they got home tonight. They stood with their shoulders hunched, tapping thick blue clay from their boots onto the wet plywood floor. Not a smile in the room. Nobody wanted to be here, but the damp and the grime and the English foreman were to be tolerated, if you wanted beer money. The old boy in front of Nial hocked a glob of phlegm into the palm of his hand and ground his cigarette out in it before smearing the lot onto the leg of his pants. The coarse animal energy in the room was raw and primitive, but the food was cheap and tasty as hell.

The young Cockney girls behind the crude plywood food counter were hard as nails with tongues quicker than concord. Sue was the most brazen of the bunch, always had her blouse open an extra button or two, and winked if she caught you staring at her cleavage as she leaned over to scoop the beans onto your plate. She winked a lot. It was as much feminine warmth as many of the men would feel in a day, and they were grateful for it.

Nial felt awkward in the canteen. He was the youngest-looking worker on the site by far. A couple of other Irish lads couldn't have been much older than himself, but there was age in their eyes after a year or two of London worksites under their belts. Nial looked like a boy in comparison. The day before he'd left for London, his uncle Matt had laughed at the news.

"Can you swim that far? I don't think they let children onto a plane without an adult."

"I suppose I could stay home and do what you do… scratch my balls in front of the telly all day."

"What do you think you're gonna do over there?"

"I dunno. Joinery."

"You couldn't join your hands."

"He'll be as good a worker as any of them free-staters over there, that's for sure." His mother had interjected in his defense seeing how uncomfortable he was getting at his uncle's ball-breaking.

Then his father chimed in from behind the newspaper in the corner. "Don't know where you're runnin'. Didn't I tell you Jackie Donnelly'd give you the start in the mornin'. Ten pound a day in yer hand and Tuesday mornins off to sign on the dole. Yer not interested in work at all far as I can see."

It was bait on a stick. Nial knew that his father had gone to see Jackie Donnelly and petitioned, hat in hand, for that job for him. It was his father's last-ditch attempt to keep his only remaining son at home where he could see him. Nial's dad didn't want to see him go. None of them did. They'd lost one son to England already. One was enough. But they wouldn't say it outright. Same way he wasn't going to hear that they loved him or that they still cried for Cathal when they were alone together in their room at night. You didn't go around wearing your heart on your sleeve. It wasn't how things were done. Not in this house. Not in this country. You didn't have to go around pointing everything out with a big stick to know that it was there. You talked around a thing, you dealt with it in silence, and you let it be.

Nial couldn't tell them the real reason he was going to London. They'd know in time though. He was going to make damn sure of that.

"Are ye gunna ate that toast?" A big Irishman across from Nial at the table grunted. He pronounced it "tosht"… the "sh" was a southern thing… or a Mick-in-London thing. Nial couldn't be sure. The accent took on another layer over here. It was still English, but it was an English unrecognizable to an Englishman. Another way to keep them out.

"Naw… you can have me tosht," Nial said, laying emphasis on the "tosht," and a couple of the old boys chuckled at that. They got it. The kid was learning all right.

"What are they givin' ye after tax… in yer hand?" The big man said as a way of shifting the conversation, lifting the discomfort of the joke off of him.

"Fifty," Nial said.

"A day? Holy mother of god, d'ye hear that! Fifty pound a day for a runt of a cub."

"I'm not a runt."

"When I was yer age we'd be lucky to get cold tae, a slice of bread, and our shite home in a bag."

"If ye were lucky," said an old man with a face as sad as a small coffin. "Do yourself a favor, cub. Save every penny. Get out of this town and go on to America quick as you can, fore you turn around one day in a room all alone and realize you just drank thirty years of yer life away in the blink of an eye." The old boy stood up abruptly and walked away. A hush fell over the table. The conversation was over.

Nial had no intention of ending up like these men. He would do what he came to do as quickly as possible and get out of England again as quickly as possible. No one here even knew his real name. The foreman had called him Paddy on his first day on the site, so Nial had adopted the name as his own and nobody was any the wiser. He'd already decided to use the name Pat as an alias... but Paddy would work just as well on the building site. "Paddy the Paddy," the foreman had laughed. "Don't get any more Irish than that." "No, it doesn't." Nial had agreed. It was best no one knew his real name. It would leave it easier to cover his tracks.

The man Nial had come to take care of was Corporal Jason Anderson. Anderson had been on duty with a foot patrol of British soldiers in County Tyrone roughly a year earlier. Nial's older brother Cathal had encountered the patrol on the road somewhere outside Sixmilecross. Cathal was on his bicycle. Anderson claimed Cathal had pointed a gun at him. A gun that later turned out to be a stick. Anderson claimed he'd fired in self-defense. He was acquitted of all charges.

But Nial had read the coroner's report. Cathal had been shot in the back of the head. The family couldn't even wake him with an open coffin. The damage to his face was too traumatic, they had said.

CHURCH END

Nial had constructed his own version of the story. Cathal had encountered the British foot patrol while he was riding his bike to town. That part was true. Knowing Cathal and knowing how British soldiers treated young Catholic lads like he and Nial on a regular basis, they had most definitely stopped him and asked him a few questions. Knowing Cathal, he'd been as cheeky to the soldiers as he could be. Cathal could never gave them a straight answer. He had a quick tongue and most likely he'd humiliated Anderson in front of his pals with something he'd said. Nial had seen him do it on numerous occasions. Cathal had been fearless. Only this time Cathal was by himself. This time there wasn't another Catholic around to witness it. This time he was just another smart-ass Irishman on a quiet country road, who, in Anderson's eyes, looked like a young IRA man in the making. They'd probably let him ride away from the checkpoint. And then Anderson had shot him in the back of the head. Maybe he'd held up his rifle and leveled it at the back of Cathal's head as you might if you were at war, and you were messing around with a few of your friends. Maybe his finger had slipped on the trigger, maybe he'd just exerted a little more pressure than he'd intended. Or maybe he'd just taken aim and fired, deliberately killing his brother. It was doubtful the exact truth would ever be known… but three things were for sure:

Cathal was unarmed.

Anderson shot him in the back of the head.

Nial's only brother was dead.

After the court case, Anderson just disappeared. Nial and his parents were left to deal with the emotional carnage. But Nial couldn't let it go. If Anderson could commit murder and walk away scot-free, well then two could play at that game. If the courts couldn't serve justice, he'd do it himself.

Nial had never had a murderous bone in his body. He'd never had a single thought of joining the IRA, as many of his friends had. Nor had Cathal. But this was different. This wasn't sectarian or political. This was personal.

Chapter 2

"How're ye? Barry Callaghan. Dublin." That's how he'd introduced himself. A fag hanging from the corner of his gob, a tin of Harp in one hand and the other stuck straight out for a shake.

That's how Nial had met Barry on the day he'd left home, on the ferry ride over to Holyhead. He'd been standing on deck watching the Irish coast recede. The seagulls cawed hungrily overhead watching for scraps of food. Their wings tumbling in heavy gusts against the backdrop of a sky the color of wet cement.

Nial took his hand.

"Pat Donnelly, Tyrone." Nial had decided on the alias just before he'd boarded the bus in Ballygawley four hours earlier. It was a good Tyrone name… and it should hold up, just as long as he didn't get into a conversation with another Tyrone man who might recognize him.

"Up the Ra," Barry said, sliding a cockeyed smile in

behind it so it wouldn't be taken too seriously.

"What'd you say your name was?" said Nial.

"Barry, but call me Baz. Everybody calls me Baz."

"Isn't that a washing detergent?"

"That's me; Baz, unbeatable white." He flashed a mouthful of buckled, tar-stained teeth. "So yer off to da Big Schmoke."

Nial gave a puzzled grunt.

"The Big Smoke," Baz said. "London?"

"Oh. Aye. I'm goin' over to give it a shot for a couple of months."

"Where'ye stayin'?"

"Not sure yet."

"Whaddya mean, yer not sure yet? Do you know anybody in London?"

"Maybe."

"Maybe, he says. Do you have a job lined up?"

"Naw. But I hear there's no shortage of work, right?"

"Any gods amount of it. Here," Baz said, shoving the tin of Harp into Nial's hand, as he pulled another one from his jacket pocket. "Get this inta ye. Do ye have a pen on ye?"

"Naw."

"You're gonna be a big hit in London you are," Baz said as he walked off and started tapping people on the shoulders looking to borrow a pen. Nial watched him, half amused, half wary, you could never be sure with a Dub. But there was something instantaneously likable about this Baz character. He had long silken hair tied back in a careless ponytail, skin as pale and smooth as a china dolls, and he walked with an exaggerated spring to his step like he was forcing himself up onto his tip toes with every theatrical stride. He was like no one Nial had ever met before. But Nial reminded himself that he wasn't out to make new friends. He had a serious mission to complete. He'd take care of that and get out of London as quickly as possible.

"This is the number of a construction agency," Baz said, handing him a scrap of paper. "They're just off the North Circular. I wrote the directions on there. If you get lost, head toward Wembley."

"Thanks."

"Those guys would set you up with a job if you walked in there with a guide dog. I put the address of my local boozer on there too. If you ever need a place to stay, you come find me." Baz raised his beer. "Here's to getting out of Ireland."

The two boys tapped their beer cans and tipped them back.

Baz produced a half pint of whiskey out of his duffle bag before they got off the ferry, and they drained it between them on the train ride into London.

By the time they reached the city, they were half tore.

At Acton Town Tube station, Baz pointed at the sign for the Jubilee Line.

"This is me," he said.

Nial decided this was as good a place as any to say goodbye. "Thanks for the beer," he said.

"Come up to The White Horse one night," Baz said, "We'll have a pint."

"I will."

Baz gave Nial a friendly punch on the chest and disappeared.

Nial stepped outside the station. It was still early afternoon. He jumped into the back of a black taxi and read the driver the address off the scrap of paper Baz had given him. He was going to need a job, and money, and a roof over his head while he looked for Anderson.

"You got it guvner," the driver said in a thick Cockney accent as he read the address on the scrap of paper. "First time in London?"

"Yes."

"Come over for the work?"

"Yes."

"Whole town's full of you Irish lads. Where you from over there, North or South?"

"North. County Tyrone."

"I heard of it. Bloody Troubles. Live and let live, I say. Suppose you see a lot of that where you're from?"

Nial let the question hang in the air. He'd never been in a conversation with an Englishman in his entire life, other than a soldier at a British checkpoint. There were unspoken rules about such things. The English were not to be trusted… and there was no reason in the wide world to trust this one.

The rain had started down heavy and the afternoon had turned suddenly dark. A woman pushing a pram turned her head into the wind. A man in a suit ran by holding a newspaper up to his face. For the first time since he'd left Tyrone early that morning, Nial felt scared. What the hell had he come to London for! This was madness. What made him think he could find

Anderson? What if that wasn't even his real name? Maybe the soldiers who served in the north of Ireland used false names too. Why the hell didn't he just tag along with Baz and forget this whole damn mess?

"You alright there, guvner?"

"Aye. I'm alright."

"I said, you probably seen a lot them Troubles where youse from." He was glancing at Nial in the rearview mirror.

"Naw. Never seen any of it," Nial said.

"Wot? Really?"

"Naw. I think they probably exaggerate all that stuff in the newspapers. Great place for trout fishing though. It's lovely countryside. You should visit sometime."

The driver dropped it.

Twenty minutes later they were parked outside a two-story brick office building with a lawn sign that read, "MCLA, McGinley's Construction and Labor Agency." The sign was bracketed with two large rusty hammers.

Nial paid the driver and asked him if he knew how to get to The White Horse Tavern in Harlesden, showing him the scrap of paper Baz had given him.

"That's just a hop skip and a jump from here guv," the driver said, taking the scrap of paper and drawing Nial a quick road map. "There you go, mate."

Nial felt guilty as he took the piece of paper. The man had been courteous and sweet and he'd been an ass.

"Sorry."

"What are you sorry about?"

"I'm not used to speaking to English people."

"Thas awright. You'll get the hang of it, guvner. We're not so bad really… bit like you lot, I suppose."

Chapter 3

"Let me guess: you need a job. Here, take this… fill in your name on the top and I'll get somebody to chat to you right away. First day?" The girl behind the counter had barely looked up at Nial. Her accent was Irish, or English. Or maybe it wasn't an accent at all. It was all business. A proper accent.

"Yes, first day," Nial offered.

"Where are you from?"

"Ireland."

"Ireland?"

"Tyrone."

"Among the bushes?"

Nial wasn't sure what that meant so he let it go. She tipped her head forward and gazed at him over the top of her glasses.

"How old are you?"

"Eighteen."

"You don't look it."

"Do I have to look it?"

"Go through that door..." She snapped the sheet of paper off the desk and glanced at it for his name. "...Pat. Down the hall. Second door on the left. That's Dessie's office. He's a Tyrone man too. He'll be delighted to meet you."

Nial hadn't prepared himself for meeting another Tyrone man right out of the gate. He considered bolting for the exit. The secretary raised her eyebrow and cocked her head toward the door.

Nial went down the hall and into Dessie's office reluctantly. He stood in front of Dessie's desk trying to will himself to look older.

"Well?"

"I was told to come in here and see you."

"And?"

"And I was looking for a job?"

"You were, were you? What's your name kid?"

"Pat."

"Pat?" Dessie repeated, weighing him up.

"That's right."

"Pat, Pat, Pat. I'm Dessie. Sit down for godssake. You're looking for the schtart?" He'd emphasized the word start, making a big deal about pronouncing it "schtart."

"I was given this address by a lad I met on the ferry today. He said you might have some construction jobs available."

"What was the lad's name?"

"Barry Callaghan."

Dessie rubbed his chin and slowly shook his head.

"Never heard of him."

"Long hair," Nial continued. "From Dublin. I think he calls himself Baz."

"Oh, that little prick. Where the fuck is he? Is he in here with you?"

"Naw, I don't know where he is," Nial said, suddenly regretting mentioning Baz at all. "I don't even know him. I met him for about two minutes on the boat."

"You know where he is?"

"I don't know."

"I have a few people want to speak to that little fucker. Disappeared off a job a few weeks back, a lot of tools disappeared the same day. If you see him, tell him I'm looking for him."

"I really don't know him."

"The little cocksucker. Thinks he can steal from me!"

This interview wasn't going at all well. Dessie picked up a pencil and started tapping it loudly on the desk as he stared at Nial. Dessie was a big, no-nonsense lug of a man. Thick shoulders, no visible neck, short dark hair and hard dry eyes. Not the kind of man you'd picture sitting behind a desk.

"You sure you have no idea where to find him?"

"Not a clue."

Dessie rolled the pencil in his fingers. Nial expected it to snap at any second.

"The little wanker. I'll crack his fucken neck if I get me hands on him. Your first time away from home, Pat?"

"It is."

"Well, welcome to The Big Schmoke I suppose. You're from Tyrone, I'm guessing."

"Yes."

"A fellow countryman, huh. What part?"

"Strabane," Nial lied.

"Ah, you know Dan Lynch then?"

"No. Don't think I know him."

"Course ye do… Dan Lynch. GAA," Dessie emphasized.

"Ah. I don't follow the football," Nial said, relieved for a door out of the connection to this Dan Lynch character, but Nial could see that the way Dessie's face dropped that he might as well have announced that he liked playing dress-up with little boys. Dessie looked truly disgusted. Nial noticed a small twitch in the corner of Dessie's mouth. In the long pause that followed, Nial could hear Dessie's breathing become more labored as if he were trying to restrain himself from leaping over the desk and beating Nial to a bloody pulp.

"What do you do?" Dessie asked eventually. The chit chat was over. He wanted Nial out of his sight as quickly as possible.

"I don't know. What do you have available?"

"What d'ye mean, what do you have available?" Dessie barked.

"Well, I'm willing to work, that's all."

"Right, right…" Dessie said, composing himself. "Good man, Pat. Good man. That's the stuff. We need more good Irishmen like you over here, men willing to work. Am I right? Course I'm right. You're not another one of these Paddies who land over here and then spends the rest of his life in the bottom of a fucken pint glass are you?"

"That's definitely not me," Nial said, attempting to sound sincere.

"Good man. Good man. We have enough of them hoores around here. What kind of experience do you have?" Nial lingered long enough on the answer that Dessie just tore ahead. "You're a chippie. Am I right? We need carpenters. That alright with you?"

"Great. Yes. A chippie."

"You never worked as a carpenter a day in your life, did you?"

"My father's a carpenter," Nial offered.

"Close enough. How are you fixed for a few quid?" Dessie pulled a wad of cash from his pocket, peeled off a few twenties, and handed them to Nial. "Here, I'll deduct it from your first paycheck. Go buy yourself a tape measure and a hammer. You disappear on me like that other little cocksucker, I'll find you and wring your fucken neck. Here," he said shoving a piece of paper and a pencil at Nial, "write this down... let's see... get yerself a hammer, a handsaw, a couple of screwdrivers, a half-inch chisel, and some sort of a tool bag. You got that?" Nial nodded as he scribbled. "And rub some fucken dirt on that tool bag when you get it, try to make it look like you didn't just fall off the boat altogether. You got it?"

"Got it," Nial said handing him back the pencil.

"No... keep it, you'll need that too. Where are you staying?"

"Harlesden," Nial said giving him the only semblance of an address that he had. "Near The White Horse."

"That other wee fucker was staying over that direction too."

"Who?"

"That long-haired Dublin cunt."

"Oh?"

"You sure you don't know where he is?"

Nial shook his head. Dessie sighed loudly and let it go.

"I'll have a man pick you up in front of The White Horse at seven o'clock in the morning. He'll be in a blue van. Don't be late."

"You can count on me, Dessie," Nial said, standing up.

Nial deduced from the cold, dead-eyed stare directed at him from the far side of the desk that Dessie would never forgive him for not liking football.

Chapter 4

"It's the terrorist," Baz yelled as soon as he spotted Nial standing in the door of The White Horse pub carrying a brand-new white canvas tool bag.

"Marty," Baz yelled, turning to the bartender. "Two pints, and a couple of vodkas, please. This man looks like he's ready to build something, he'll need a good stiff drink at once."

Marty, a short angry barrel of a man, cursed under his breath and limped off down the bar to fetch the drinks.

"That's Marty, he's an angry little bastard, he's got a gimp leg and a fast right hand," Baz said, as Nial stepped up to the bar next to him.

The Baz was glassy-eyed and slurring, but Nial was relieved to find him in any state at all. It was getting dark out and Baz was the only person Nial knew in this whole damn town.

"So you stopped at McGinley's?" Baz said, pointing

at the clean tool bag.

Nial nodded, deciding not to bother mentioning that Dessie was looking for him. Whatever beef Dessie and Baz had was between them. It was just good to see a familiar face.

"Here, ya dumb fucker, two pints, two vodkas," Marty the bartender grumbled as he set the drinks in front of the lads before snapping a tenner from Baz's hand.

"Marty," Baz said to the bartender. "Meet Pat."

"Great. Another fucken Mick. Just what we fucken needed in this town," Marty barked as he hobbled off to the cash register.

Baz raised his glass aloft. "To Paddies and Micks everywhere."

Nial lifted a vodka and joined the toast. "To the Paddies."

"Two more vodkas Marty," Baz called.

"What'd your last fucken slave die of, cunt…. asshole…" Marty spat.

"Marty is the sole reason I love this establishment," Baz offered sincerely.

Despite Marty's gruff demeanor, The White Horse was much more homely than Nial had anticipated on the walk from McGinley's office. Two high-backed orange velvet armchairs sat in front of an open-hearth fire. A few civilized-looking locals occupied the booths around the pool table in the back and a row of red tasseled wall sconces gave the place a soft homely vibe. To Nial's surprise there seemed to be as many English accents in the bar as Irish. No one seemed to give a shit. It was the first time he'd ever been in a social situation with an English person. Back in Tyrone this was a definite no-no. Catholics drank in Catholic bars and Protestants drank in theirs. Nial wasn't about to go buying any of them a pint in a hurry, but as long as they left him alone, he was pretty sure he could abide their presence for the evening. The vodkas were working too of course, and Nial felt some sort of warmth working its way into his bones for the first time since he'd left Tyrone.

"Dinner!" Baz announced, holding a thin, dignified finger in the air. "Let's get you fed before we get you loaded.

"Sandra, darling," he said, stopping a waitress passing by with a tray of creamy pints of Guinness. "Two of your finest shepherd's pies, toute suite."

"What'd you say about my fanny?" Sandra said as she gave Pat a playful wink. "Should I bring more than one fork?"

"Don't mind Sandra. She hasn't been laid for a decade or so."

"I'd be a long time waiting for a decent shag in this kip. Two shepherd's pies coming right up."

"I'll shag you, so I will," slurred a big grimy Irish lad who was sitting within earshot of the conversation at the bar.

"I rest my case," Sandra said, as she sailed away with her tray.

"Pat, meet Donald," said Baz, turning to the lad. "Or, as we like to call him around here... So I Will."

"Fuck you, you jackeen cunt," Donald barked. "I'll take the fucken head off ye with a schlap, so I will, so I will."

Nial had to stifle a laugh.

"Who's this hoore?" Donald said, turning on his stool to get a good look at Nial.

"This is Pat from Tyrone."

"First day in The Big Schmoke?"

"First day."

"I'll buy you a pint then so... so I will... so I will."

But before he could get Marty's attention, Donald seemed to drift off into another world. He swayed a little on the stool, almost toppled over, then he just stood bolt up, and marched out the door. And he was gone.

"What the hell happened there?" Nial asked.

"Don't worry about that boy," said Baz. "So I Will landed in this town with only ten quid in his pocket, didn't know a sinner, bit like you... couldn't read or write a word of English..."

"I can read," Nial said, but Baz went on with his story.

"... walked into the first bar he saw and drank the tenner right off the bat. End of the night some fella asks him if he can drive. That's how he got his first job driving a lorry. Lived in the cab of that truck for six months."

"How'd he get around if he couldn't read the street signs?" Nial asked.

"He stopped and asked for directions. Pretty soon he knew the whole city like the back of his hand. Still can't read or write a word but he's managed to buy himself three houses back at home, has them all rented out... makin' an absolute fortune... no flies on So I Will."

It was true, Nial thought, the streets of London really were paved with gold. If a guy like So I Will could make a go of it, then there was hope for just about anybody. Maybe he should forget about finding Anderson and just focus on the work. God knows his family could use all the financial help they could get.

But he no sooner had the thought til he hated himself for it. Here he was, first day in England, and already he was getting sidetracked with booze and money. He set the last of his pint down and shook his head. He had to stay focused.

The door to the bar opened and a crowd of leather-clad bikers and their girls stumbled in.

"Look at this crowd?" said Baz, nodding to the door. Three of the girls stopped with Baz. One of them kissed him playfully on the cheek, the second girl discreetly slipped something into his jeans pocket and whispered, "You fucken owe me for the last one too."

The prettiest of the bunch draped her arm around Baz's shoulders and stared inquisitively at Nial. Nial's chest tightened and his face flushed. She was just about as beautiful a girl as he'd ever met. She had long chestnut brown hair and dark brown eyes that glistened when she smiled, and right now she was smiling at Nial's obvious discomfort.

"Where'd you find this one?" she asked.

"On the ferry this morning. This is Pat. Pat... Marissa."

"Your mother know you're out this late?" Marissa teased as she cocked her head at Nial waiting for a response, but he didn't have one. He was speechless. Her smile brightened a little more as if she'd read something that had been penciled on wall of his heart. She turned and she was gone with the rest of the crowd to the pool table in the back.

"Who was that?" Nial asked taking a sip of his pint, trying to mask his instantaneous attraction to her.

"That's Marissa. She's a gee bag."

"A what?"

"A gee bag… she'll wreck yer fucken head man. Stay the fuck away from that crowd. Nothin' but trouble."

"She's beautiful."

"London's full of beautiful women. They're a dime a dozen in this town, me auld tosser."

Nial let it go.

"So, you need a place to stay. Am I right?" Baz asked. Nial nodded. "No sweat man, you can bunk at my gaff."

"Cheers, Baz."

"Place is a kip but it's dry, and it's free."

"Free?"

"Don't worry, Pat. I'll look out for ya."

For the first time, Nial felt the sting when Baz called him Pat. Here was a lad who was helping him out, an honest to goodness decent sod, trying to be his friend, and here he was lying to him.

"I should probably get back and get some sleep," Nial said. "They're picking me up at seven outside here in the morning and I'm about wrecked."

Baz drained the last of his pint in a swallow. "Let's go."

The two boys were a few blocks from The White Horse when Baz stopped suddenly. "Shit. That reminds me: you need a bed."

They were standing outside a furniture store. In the window was a full bedroom display. Without another word, Baz lifted a trash can and flung it through the large window; the huge pane shattered all over the sidewalk, and an alarm system began to wail.

"What are you doing?" Nial said, flabbergasted, but Baz was already stepping through the shattered glass and retrieving the single mattress off the bed frame. He got it out onto the street in a flash and balanced it on his head.

"Feels soft," Baz said, seeming quite satisfied with his haul. "C'mon... run."

The Baz started running. He was surprisingly nimble for a drunk with a mattress on his head. Nial, not knowing quite how to respond to the situation, followed him across the dual carriageway toward the drab housing estate on the far side. Nial grabbed the rear end of the mattress as they ducked down a narrow alleyway between two buildings. A police siren could be heard rapidly approaching. Baz dodged into a dark, urine-smelling stairwell and Nial followed him up two flights of stairs to a flat at the very end of the balcony. Baz propped the mattress against the railing for a moment, found the key, and in a flash they were inside.

"Leave the lights off for now til the cops clear," Baz said, as he dragged the mattress through the short hallway and dropped it on the living room floor. He reached in his breast pocket and produced a ready rolled joint, holding it up for Nial to see. He struck a match and stepped to the big living room window as he fired it up.

"Whose house is this?" Nial asked.

"Mine, and yours."

"How much?"

"I told you, it's free. Squatters rights. Welcome to Church End Estate… and now you have a lovely new bed, and a room of your very own to put it in. I never use this fucken room anyway. Throw your own lock on the door if you like."

"You're nuts," Nial said, taking a glance around the cluttered living room as his eyes adjusted to the yellow streetlight streaming in from Church Road. There was a record player on a shelf in the corner, a couple of big speakers, a ripped poster of Billy Idol sellotaped to the wallpaper, a beat-up couch, and a couple of old armchairs. It had a door and a window. It was dry and warm. It was just about perfect as far as Nial was concerned. Beyond the window the flashing lights of the police car could be seen racing past on Church Road.

Baz passed Nial the joint as he stepped to the window beside him.

"What's in that?"

"Don't tell me you never smoked a little hash."

Nial shook his head.

"Don't worry, it'll not do you a button of harm."

He was standing in a squat in London with a complete stranger who'd just robbed a furniture store. Nial didn't have a single reason in the world to trust this person. He took the joint from Baz and took a good long hit and they stood together in the darkened living room watching the flashing lights of the cop cars assemble outside the furniture store across the dual carriageway.

Chapter 5

"You call this straight, do ya?" Harry spat as he held a four-foot spirit level to the doorframe Nial had just hung. "I've seen pigs' dicks straighter than this fucken doorframe."

Nial could see that the door was out maybe two millimeters in the four-foot span that the level covered. It was nothing really in the grand scheme of things, but Harry was right, it wasn't perfect, and as rough as the Irish chippies on the site might appear, they held themselves to impossible standards when it came to their work.

The Burner glanced over Harry's shoulder with his one good eye at the thin line of daylight between the frame and the spirit level.

"He's right. There's a gee hair in it," said The Burner.

"I'll fix it," Nial said.

"You're bloody right you'll fix it," Harry barked. "If I see you hang another doorframe like that on my site, you can pack your shit and get the fuck out of here...

you hear me. Paddy?"

Nial popped a nail-bar behind the frame and went about straightening it.

In the short while he'd been working as a carpenter, Nial had improved remarkably. So much so that the task of hanging the doorframes had fallen almost entirely to him. He had a good eye and patience for the work. With the generous tutelage of The Burner, Nial had learned more about being a carpenter than he would have in four years of serving an apprenticeship back home. There the old tradesmen had a system of prolonged torture for the young trainees. You could have been an apprentice carpenter for a year back in Tyrone and still been considered little more than a tea boy. Certainly no one would have trusted you with a hammer and chisel to tackle an oak doorframe. But here in London the old rules did not apply. There was no time. If you wanted carpenter's wages you better learn to do what carpenters do, in a hurry.

The site at Kings Cross covered about four acres of ground. It was to be a new library. Hundreds of men from all over Europe were employed on the site but the bulk of the labor was Irish. Almost all of the foremen were English. There were only a couple of Irish foremen. Nial had been warned to watch out for them. There was only one thing worse than an English foreman, and that was an Irishman who'd kissed enough English ass to achieve that status.

Nial had been paired with The Burner on the first day on the site. Harry had taken one look at Nial when he had arrived with his clean tool bag and simply shook his head. John The Burner happened to be walking by and had stepped in to vouch for Nial out of the blue.

"He can work with me."

"He's twelve," Harry had said.

"I'm eighteen," said Nial.

"If he fucks up a doorframe you can take it out of my wages," offered The Burner.

"Alright… get him out of my sight. He's your problem now."

The Burner was from Tuam. He'd been a woodwork teacher for fifteen years in a high school in Galway. He understood teenagers and he had the patience to deal with mistakes. He was as thin as a reed, balding on top, with an unruly gray mustache. He was slow and methodical in his work. For John The Burner, everything was a procedure. He spent twenty minutes every morning, on his own time, organizing his tool belt for the day's work. Everything had to be just so, every tool had its slot, every screw had its special place.

Burner approached every project with the same level of attention. He was the real deal, a true craftsman. When The Burner was finished working on a project, you could rest assured it was done.

He'd spent those first few days with Nial teaching him the importance of safety and pace on the job. He tutored Nial on the finer elements of the craft like the importance of owning and caring for a proper oil stone. A good craftsman might sharpen his chisel five or six times a day if he was working with a hardwood like oak. He showed Nial how to dismantle a wood plane and give it an edge sharp enough to shave with.

"If it's not sharp enough to shave the hair off a fly's balls without nicking the skin, go back to the stone with it," he had said. "If in doubt, snare a fly, and give its nuts a run of the blade."

As they worked, The Burner pried Nial for information on his background. When he sensed Nial didn't want to talk about it, he'd let it go. He had a solid respect for secrecy. He also seemed keen to tutor Nial on the politics and dynamics of their work situation.

"Dessie Doyle. Now there's a man to keep your eyes peeled for. I never trust a man with eyes like a shark. You can be sure they look that way for a reason."

"He trusted me enough to give me the start," said Nial in defense.

"He's fond enough of you Northerners alright, but he has less time for us free-staters, and even less time again for the English. You ever see Harry when he's around? They're afraid of him around here. It's rumored he killed a British soldier about fifteen years ago, caved his head in with a lump hammer. They never found proof to pin it on him proper, but he done ten years in the Kesh over it just the same."

"Why'd he kill him?"

"Story was, the soldier was sneaking off the base nightly to visit Dessie's younger sister. Dessie come up on him from behind one night out of the bushes with the lump hammer and put an end to it. Don't mess with Dessie. He's a mystery man and best left that way. He's connected… he knows people… knows how to get things done, or un-done."

Nial didn't ask for details. If The Burner said he was

connected, you could rest assured Dessie was connected. The Burner was a man who knew what was what. He had the quiet air of authority about him. Nial knew that as long as he was under The Burner's wing, Harry the foreman would tolerate his inexperience. Everybody on the site held The Burner in high regard, which gave Nial a wonderful sense of protection.

Nial was two weeks in London already, and he was still no closer to finding Anderson. He had just about exhausted any plans he'd had to track him down. He'd spent hours poring through the phone book, but there were pages upon pages of Andersons to choose from. If he were listed, it was likely under an alias. He'd visited seven or eight addresses, but no one he tracked down looked remotely like the man he sought. He had underestimated the complexity of finding a complete stranger in a city of seven million people. But in the meantime he was inadvertently learning a trade, an unexpected bonus. He also found to his surprise that he liked being away from home. He liked it a lot, truth be told. He liked squatting in Church End Estate with The Baz. He liked The White Horse Tavern and the locals he met there. He liked smoking a little hash. He liked that the Jamaicans had taken him into the fold. He enjoyed sharing a joint with them on occasion. He enjoyed the feeling of a life that existed outside of Northern Ireland, outside of The Troubles. Another life was unfolding here, a life that felt roomier than the one he left behind, but still, he kept a part of himself locked away from it all.

He had come here for one reason. He would find

Anderson and kill him. When he was done, he would leave London, and everyone in it without a thought.

Chapter 6

"Ah, it's you again. They give you the road already?" It was Mary. Dessie's secretary at McGinley's.

"The road?" asked Nial.

"Did they chase you off the job already?"

"No... I..." Nial began, but the phone rang and Mary answered it before he could defend himself. Nial had decided he needed help in tracking down Anderson. And after what The Burner had told him about Dessie, he decided it was time to take a chance on asking for help. If Dessie went ballistic on him, well then he would just walk away from his job with McGinley's, get another job, and start over. Keep going.

Mary cupped her hand over the receiver. "Sorry, what'd you say you wanted?"

"Is Dessie here?"

Mary raised an arm, pointed Nial in the general direction of Dessie's office, and went back to her conversation.

The door to Dessie's office was open. Nial gave it a knock as he entered. Dessie was behind the desk, doing nothing.

"Pat? Am I right?" Dessie said, a furrow deep as a potato drill weighing heavily over his eyelids. "The lad who doesn't like football."

"That's me," Nial admitted reluctantly as he closed the door behind him.

"Somebody dead?"

"What?"

"You here to bring me bad news?"

"No. Not really."

"Spit it out then. Let's hear it."

"I need some help."

"I fucken knew it. What about the hundred I gave you already, and your wages? I knew from the minute I saw you, you were a fucken druggie. What kind of a queer doesn't like football? A fucken drug addict, that's who…"

"I'm not a druggie… I don't need money…"

"I've no fucken LSD in here for you, boy, if that's what you're looking for."

"I heard that you might be the man to come see."

"You what?"

"I heard that you were the man to see if I needed something done," Nial said hurriedly, and immediately regretted uttering the words. This was insanity. Dessie was an unhinged lunatic. He was liable to leap across the table and strangle him on the spot. But he didn't. Instead, he stopped. Furrowed his brow further.

"Who said, what?"

"I just heard that I might be able to come talk to you… about something."

"About what exactly?"

"I'm looking for somebody."

"Oh, you are, are you? Who?"

"I need to find a man here in London… and if you help me, I'll pay you."

Dessie chuckled.

"I have some money saved," Nial added.

"I see. And who's this man you're looking for?"

"Are you going to help me?"

"I don't know yet. Who is he?"

"Just a man."

"Aha… and what are you going to do with this man when you find him?"

"That's my business. I just need to know if you can help me. If you can't I'll just leave."

Dessie leaned back a little in his seat. Nial watched him make strange shapes with mouth as if he were washing his teeth with the idea. He leaned forward again and shook a cigarette out of a box and lit it before throwing the box to Nial and nodding for him to sit. Nial sat down across from him and took a smoke from the box and lit it.

"I suppose I need to know what's in it for me if I help you with this thing, Pat."

"I told you," Nial said. "I'll pay you."

"I heard you. But I don't really need your money, do I?" Dessie said.

Nial let it hang. He could see Dessie was working this through some sort of internal abacus. There would be a price alright, but it would be on Dessie's terms. "Besides, if I give you some information… if I decide to help you out, I would need some sort of insurance. I barely even know you. You know what I mean? We have to come to some sort of a mutual understanding. A show of faith, if you will."

"So what do you want from me?" Nial asked, a little relieved that at least he wasn't getting his skull smashed into a filing cabinet.

"A favor," Dessie said.

"What sort of favor?"

"I don't know yet…. But let's just say I know some people, and once in a while they might need a little something or other taken care of."

"I'm not gay," Nial said.

"Who said you were fucken gay?"

"You did."

"Did I? Oh right. No. It's not that. Are you gay?"

"No, Dessie, I'm not gay."

"Jesus, settle down a wee bit there, Paddy. It's a civil fucken question. No need to get your knickers in a bunch. No, it's not that kind of a favor."

"So what is it then?"

Dessie settled his elbows on the desk and studied Nial's face for what seemed like a very long time. He stared deep into Nial's eyes and grunted and moaned as if he were clearing his throat or swallowing a small hedgehog. Then, keeping him fixed in his gaze, he spoke in a low growl.

"You're from the North, Pat… a good Catholic lad… I don't need to spell this shit out for you. We do you a favor, you do us a favor. You see what I'm saying?"

Nial nodded, though in truth he wasn't quite sure what Dessie was saying. Was Dessie IRA? Or was he something more sinister? Nial hoped he wouldn't be around London long enough to find out. He'd take what information Dessie had to offer on Anderson, do what he came to do, and get out of town as quickly as possible before Dessie and his people came after him.

"I'm trying to find a British soldier," Nial said, getting to the point. "Corporal Jason Anderson. He's about fifty-five years old. He was in the North until about a year ago. I believe he's living in London. But that's all I know."

Dessie mouthed the name as he scribbled it on a writing pad.

"What'd he do, this Anderson?"

Nial said nothing. The corners of Dessie's mouth curled up ever so slightly into a sick smile. He was looking at Nial now like he owned him.

"You leave it to me, kid. I'll find this fucker for you."

"Thanks," Nial said, as he stood and turned for the door. He felt suddenly claustrophobic, like he'd stumbled into the tangle of a fisherman's net. He wanted to get out of there and as far away from Dessie as possible.

"Hey, Pat."

Nial stopped, his hand on the door.

"Just remember… you're gonna owe us after this."

Chapter 7

By the time Nial had walked back to Church End Estate it was almost seven thirty. The sun had tapered off beyond the world, leaving a dying orange glow awash over the tops of the somber little townhouses on Neasden Lane. Saint Mary's Church loomed at the top of the hill, casting an ominous shadow over its own small graveyard as he passed.

Nial stopped for the first time to look up at the centuries old church; the heavy slate roof, the rusty weather vane atop the bold stone turret, the elaborate stained glass windows. Only now did it occur to him that this was where the housing estate had gotten its name: Church End.

The ancient oak doors swung open and a young vicar stepped out in his long gray garb. He stood for a moment, his eyes closed, hands clasped as if in prayer, letting the afternoon sun bathe his face. He turned suddenly, conscious that he was being watched, and caught Nial staring at him from the other side of the low fence.

"A beautiful evening," he called.

"It's lovely, Father. Lovely to see it." Nial dipped his head, turned quickly, and continued on his way. He'd never spoken to a Protestant minister before. He'd called him Father. Protestants weren't Father... were they? He'd been caught off guard. It had only been a polite acknowledgement of the weather and yet he was consumed with a sickening sense of guilt. Here he was in England, not two wet days, and already he was making small talk with the Protestant clergy. Back in the North of Ireland the division was not just Irish against the English, it was Catholic against Protestant. It was a sectarian divide, straight down the middle... there was no gray area in the middle... and here he was casually fraternizing with the enemy. He tried to shake it off. Part of him understood that there was nothing wrong with being polite. It was a simple remark in passing. No one had even witnessed the exchange. But a deeper part of him, a part stained with the blood of ten centuries of oppression, perpetual war with the English, and the death of his brother, twisted in his gut like a knife.

He physically shook his head to rid himself of the voice. It would not be shook. He stopped and turned his face again to the last of the dropping sun. He felt the warm glow of it on his whole body. It was warmer here in England. They even had the goddamned weather, he thought. He looked down at what he was wearing: a thick canvas jacket, dirty jeans, heavy work boots. No wonder he was sweating. It was the uniform of his father. The badge of the working class. The thought of his father brought its own sense of shame.

In his pocket Nial had over two hundred pounds folded in crisp twenties; wages from a full week of work on the site. It was an astronomical paycheck for an eighteen-year-old boy with practically no carpentry skills. Nial's father had worked as a carpenter for the same local contractor for over thirty years back home in Tyrone, and he still wasn't earning even a quarter of that. It saddened Nial to think of it, and it made him ache for the hardships that his father had endured as a working class Catholic in Northern Ireland... a decent, hard working man, doing the right thing, trying to raise a family. Was this too, a part of it — the financial oppression? Here he was only a couple of hours from home, doing exactly the same job his father was doing back home in Northern Ireland, and yet he was out-earning him by about four hundred percent already. The pay difference alone might be enough to drive a man to murder.

He turned again to look at Church End Estate. His new home. It was a drab, sprawling, pre-fab ghetto, erected sometime shortly after the bombing of Hitler's War. Rows and rows of two-story dwellings sat on top of one another. Shuttered concrete stairwells climbed to the second floor balconies... balconies littered in trash and carelessly hung laundry. Weeds flourished where they could. Cracked windows were patched with cardboard or plywood. There were a thousand alleys. A thousand places for a thief to stand in the shadows with a knife. The Baz had given him fair warning to watch his back even in daylight around here. The estate crawled

CHURCH END

the entire length of Church Road, all the way to The White Horse Tavern at the foot of the road. Two square miles of concentrated sadness.

The houses were government owned. The occupants were for the most part on public assistance, lower class: Caribbeans, Pakistanis, Irish, and English. The local council had moved in to try and clean the place up, but they were battling a relentless infestation of squatters. Nial was astounded at how easy it was to live here rent-free. Here in England, you could break into an unoccupied house, put your own lock on the door, jimmy-rig the power box and the gas line, and claim the place as your own until such times as the court fought to have you legally evicted. If you could get into a place and lay claim to it for two days before the bailiff showed up, it was yours for months before they could legally kick you out. If this were back in Tyrone, the cops would simply show up at the door, smash your head in, and throw you into the street. It seemed too good to be true. There was definitely a different set of laws here on the mainland, as the British referred to jolly old England.

The majority of the squatters in Church End Estate were Irish. There were mobs of Irish in every corner. They were dug in deep. It must have presented an enormous security concern for the local authorities. These were hard-core bikers and traveling men... headbangers from the Bogside in Derry, skinheads from The Falls Road in Belfast. And of course you had the hard-core Provo contingent from East Tyrone.

In the short time Nial had been in London he'd met most of them. There was a party practically every night in somebody's squat. Although "party" might be too fine a term. Every night after Marty kicked the crowd to the curb from The White Horse Tavern, around eleven p.m., a few cases of beer and bottles of cheap gut-rot wine were organized, and the crowd convened in one squat or another, to listen to music, smoke weed, and get generally bombed out of their skulls. In appearance they were the kind of crowd you might cross the street to avoid, but many were some of the sweetest people Nial had ever met. The Irish in North London looked out for one another for the most part, just as long as you didn't cross them. You could rest assured nobody was going to be let starve to death or sleep out in the cold on the estate. Somebody was always willing to hook you up with a meal, or a couch to crash on, or another job… if you wanted one.

Nial had attended a few of the parties on his first nights in town. Baz had dragged him along. It was what people did. Nial didn't want to get too familiar with the locals. But he went in the hope that he might see Marissa again. He'd been looking out for her since that first night, but she seemed to have disappeared. Nial wasn't sure if she had a boyfriend among the biker crowd so he didn't want to raise any red flags, or get his head cracked open with a tire iron, by enquiring about her.

The Baz was popular among the locals. He stayed afloat by dodging and weaving. Though he didn't like to think of himself as a drug dealer, he did seem to sell quite a lot of hash. He'd buy an ounce and cut six quarters out of it. He could sell an ounce a day around the estate without breaking his stride. No one seemed to mind his small measures. Apparently Baz had a secret connection to the best hash in London. Nial had heard lads compare his hash to pure black opium.

Nial spotted Baz the minute he rounded the corner out of Reade Walk. He was out on the balcony with his feet up on the railing. He had the speakers from the stereo system dragged out there with him and he was blasting Pink Floyd's *The Wall*, loud enough for Nial to hear it from three hundred yards away. He appeared, even from this distance, to be enveloped in a cloud of thick smoke.

He held a bottle of wine out to Nial as he approached.

"Here, you look like you had a hard day at the office." Nial took it and tipped it to his head.

"Oh man, what is this shit?"

"Thunderbird. A fine vintage from the vineyards of somewhere or other. Only a pound a bottle, me auld sod. Hang on to that one, I've got more here." The Baz reached into a paper bag next to his armchair and produced another bottle of the ghastly brew.

"It's fucken rat poison, that's what it is," Nial said.

"Rats wouldn't touch it. Here get that into you too," Baz said, handing Nial an enormous spliff.

"You sure you should be out here smoking this while you're blasting Pink Floyd for the whole neighborhood to hear?"

"This is my kingdom, you fool. What savage would dare protest?"

"The cops… maybe."

"Nonsense. I forbid it."

"You celebrating something this afternoon? Big day at the dole office?"

"They almost had me today, the bastards. They were waiting for me when I went in, the swine. Minute I put my hand to sign the form, I seen them comin', out of the corner of my eye. Two plain clothes lads."

"How did you get away?"

"Legged it."

"Were they on crutches?"

"They were fast… but I was faster. I smoked right past them… zoom." Baz jumped up and whooshed his hand by Nial's nose. "Like fucken lightning man."

"I'm having trouble with the visual if you don't mind me saying so. You don't look like a 'zoom' kind of guy to me."

"It's the reflexes, man. I have these hypersensitive fucken reflexes. I'm like a highly advanced piece of machinery when it comes to that shit… whoosh."

"So if you didn't get your dole check, how the hell are you so flush?"

"The Baz always has a little stashed away for the rainy day me auld mucker." Baz grinned and tipped the Thunderbird to his head.

A blue Ford Escort pulled into the cracked parking lot and the two boys watched as an attractive blonde stepped from the car. She looked up at the source of the music and smiled at Nial and The Baz, and raising her fist in the air in approval, before locking her car and disappearing in the opposite direction.

CHURCH END

"Wow," Nial whispered. "You see that?"

"She was alright I suppose."

"What! You're joking, right? She was beautiful."

"You need to get laid, man," Baz drawled.

"And you don't?"

The Baz seemed to drift off. He lifted the bottle again to his lips and leaned back in his chair, closing his eyes and letting the music carry him off.

"Hey," Nial said, nudging him with his toe. "I'm talking to you."

"What do you want?" The Baz said, taking a deep drag of the spliff without ever opening his eyes.

"Hi, don't pass out on me here. I just got here. Talk to me. Tell me a story."

"What story?"

"Any story. A love story. Surely The Baz has a love story!"

"You want me to tell you a love story?"

"Yes, tell me a love story."

"Alright. I was fifteen years old. It was a lovely Saturday afternoon in Saint Stephen's Green. You know where Saint Stephen's Green is right?"

"Yeah, it's in Dublin... we used to sneak in there when we were down at —"

"Wow, wow, wow... who's telling the story here?"

"Sorry, your highness... continue."

"Your highness..." The Baz chortled at that. "Good one, man. Anyway... it was a Saturday evening, perfect weather, all that shit, and I'm strollin' along on me Tobler, and here comes —"

"Your what?"

"What?"

"You said, you were strolling along on your 'tobler'?"

"I was on me Toblerone, man… on me own… Tobler."

"Ah."

"So there I was, on me Tobler, Saturday evening in the park and here's this beauty, I mean the most gorgeous woman I've ever seen in me life, right, just sittin' on a bench…"

"On her Tobler?"

"Yeah, all by herself… you takin' the piss?"

"No. Continue."

"So I walk right over and I say, 'How's it goin, luv. Baz Daly, Dublin's Don Juan,' and without missin' a beat, she says, 'Emeralda Maltinado, Argentina's Cleopatra.'"

"You're full of shit."

"I swear, man, that's what she said. Then she just stood up and planted one on me."

"She kissed you?"

"I swear man, it was like she was just sittin' there all day waiting for me to stroll along, dirty big tongue down me throat. Took me to a hotel, pays for it on the spot, and that was it… Bob's yer uncle."

"I don't believe it. How old was she?"

"Thirty. Thirty-one. Then right afterwards she takes me over to this pub in Templebar. She gets the drinks in, and says, 'I've got to use the restroom, I'll be right back.' And that was it, never seen her again."

"She disappeared?"

"Like a ghost. I'm sitting there for like a half hour, nothing. Gone."

"What you do?"

"Finished the drinks and fucked off."

"That's a pretty spectacular story."

"Your turn."

"Well, I don't have one that's that exciting."

"Let's hear it."

"Well, I was drunk. She was drunk. It was cold. We were outside. I came. She giggled. And I made it back inside before last call."

The Baz burst out laughing. "Now that's a love story. Here's to love." He raised his bottle of Thunderbird and Nial clinked his against it. Baz took a deep pull and jumped up and surprised Nial with a bear hug.

"Right, me and you are goin out and we're getting locked."

"Sounds like the perfect plan, Don Juan."

Chapter 8

"How's it goin'?" It was Marissa. She'd slipped up behind Nial and Baz at the bar. Her hair was tied back in a ponytail and she was wearing a white t-shirt with the words "EAT ME" in bold red print across her chest.

"Nice shirt," Baz sneered.

"I know. Real class, right! Had to borrow it from Decco. All me own stuff's in the laundromat across the street." Marissa stuck her hands deep in her back pockets and cocked her head sideways at Nial with that same curious look she had given him when they first met.

"How's the new kid in town? Staying out of trouble, I hope?"

Nial smiled in response and felt himself blush.

"Go on. I'll let you buy me a drink."

"Yes. I'll buy you a drink," Nial said, a little more enthusiastically than he'd intended. Baz gave him a disappointed glance.

"I'll have a gin and bitters, thanks," Marissa said,

perching her arm on Nial's shoulder as he shot his hand up to catch Marty's attention.

"What?" Marty barked.

"A gin and bitters and two more beers, please."

"I'll fucken give you a fucken gin and bitters, dumb cunt, fucken bastard..." Marty mumbled as he hobbled off.

"Thanks Marty... Nice to see you too," Marissa called after him before turning her attention back to Nial. "So, what have you been up to?"

"I'm working as a carpenter, for McGinley's."

"Mmm, okay, so you're in London... and you're working. What else have you been up to?"

Nial shrugged.

"What's your story, Pat?"

"What do you mean?"

"I don't know. There's something you're not telling me." She was staring right into him, searching for something, and Nial had a strong feeling that she could see all the way down into the most secretive corners of his soul; all the way to that murderous stain on his heart. He could feel his face flush as he looked down at his hands to avoid her gaze.

"Leave him alone," Baz snapped. "Go pick on somebody else." Marissa ignored him. Marty set the drinks up in front of them, roughly snapping the tenner out of Nial's hand.

"Why don't you ask me something about me?" Marissa nudged, looking to get Nial back into the conversation. "Ask me anything." Nial raised his head and composed himself.

"Okay. How do you like London?" he asked her.

"It's better than home. Next."

"What do you do when you're not in here torturing people?"

Marissa smiled brightly. "There you are. I'm a secretary in a scrap-metal yard over by Neasden."

"How do you like that?"

"I'm bored out of me hole with it to be honest."

"Must be tough dealing with all those men traipsing in and out of there all day?" The Baz interjected. Marissa just went on ignoring him. She was focused fully on Nial. She lifted her drink and drained it in a swallow and gave her head a playful shake.

"Right. I better be getting back to my dirty laundry. Thanks for the drink, Pat. What are you doin' later?"

"Home, probably. Work in the morning."

"Jesus, Isn't that exciting! There's a few of us heading to The Mean Fiddler later, good band on tonight. You should come."

"I don't know…"

"Suit yourself." She leaned over and kissed his cheek and she was gone again.

"Fucken tease," Baz said as she slipped out the door.

"I think she's nice."

"You think her boobs are nice. She's got you wrapped around her little finger."

"She's beautiful."

"She's a slut."

"What's your fucken problem, man?" Nial startled himself at how bitterly he'd just snapped at The Baz in her defense. He could see he'd really hurt him too, so he blundered on, brushing it out of the way. "Come on... get that beer into you. Marty... two more whiskeys up here, pronto."

"Don't you fucken pronto me you filthy Mick bastard," Marty spat before going off to get the drinks. Baz laughed, got up, and went off toward the restroom.

Through the window Nial caught a glimpse of Marissa in the laundromat on the far side of the street. She was loading coins into a dryer in the lighted window. It took everything he had to restrain himself from racing out of the bar to run over there and tell her that he hadn't be able to stop thinking about her for five minutes since the last time he saw her.

"Come on," Baz said stepping back to the bar and lifting his glass. "Let's get these into us and get the flock outta here. I need a spliff."

Nial reluctantly went along. It was the smart thing to do. It was bad enough that he'd become so friendly with The Baz. That alone was going to make a clean getaway out of London more complicated. The last thing on earth he needed right now was to fall for Marissa too.

The two boys left the bar and headed back up Church Road. The Baz lit a spliff and draped his arm around Nial's shoulder as he launched into a raucous rendition of a rebel song they both knew well.

"Armored cars and tanks and guns, came to take away our sons, but every man must stand behind the men behind the wire."

Nial took the spliff and joined in:

"Through the little streets of Belfast, in the dark of early morn,

British soldiers came marauding, wrecking little homes with scorn.

Heedless of the children crying, dragging fathers from their beds,

Beating sons while helpless mothers, watched the blood pour from their heads."

Chapter 9

"Mum."

"Nial. Is that you? You had us worried sick. Your father's on the verge of calling the police to file a missing persons report. Are you alright?"

Nial had called her from a phone box on the street just outside Kings Cross Tube station.

It was a Saturday afternoon. He'd taken the Saturday shift just to get out of the squat for the day. He'd found that if he wasn't working he was spending more and more time in the pub getting loaded with The Baz.

"I'm fine. I told you I mightn't call for a wee while or so."

"A wee while? I thought you were dead."

"It took some time getting settled in. How are you and Dad?"

"You had us worried sick, my head was nearly away with it, what if something's happened, sure I don't even know where to look for you. Where would I start? I had you dead and buried... drowned, and shot, and stabbed... run over in the street with a bus... for the love of God, Nial, you had me sick to me stomach." His mother's voice was quivering. It had been wrong not to call her sooner. Her nerves were completely shot since Cathal's death. She didn't need to lose another son to Anderson.

"I'm sorry Mum. I won't leave it as long again."

"Where are you staying? Do you have a roof over your head at all?"

"I'm staying up in Harlesden, it's in North London. I'm sharing a place with a lad from Dublin."

"Dublin? I'd be careful of that boy if I was you. Do you have a lock on your door? Don't leave any money in the house if you're not there to keep an eye on it."

"Mum, he's a nice lad."

"They're all nice til they steal the eye out of yer head. Are you working?"

"I landed a job, first day. You can tell Dad I'm a carpenter."

"A carpenter? Sure you're not a carpenter. They'll find you out and that'll be you out of a job."

"Where's Dad? Is he there?"

"No, he's away up to Martin McCann's to get the car fixed, the exhaust fell off this evening on his way out of the town. I could hear him coming at Corrigan's. The roar of it would deafen ye. When are you coming back?"

"I told you, I just wanted to get a look at the place, see what it was like. It won't be long."

"Well, what's it like?"

"Alright, I suppose. But it's no place for an Irishman. I'll be back in a few weeks. Don't go renting my room out just yet."

"Oh don't you worry about that. Your father's expecting you back any minute I think. He was in there just this morning putting up a couple of new shelves for you… eight o'clock in the morning wrecking and banging. He landed back here yesterday with a poster for your wall…"

"A poster?"

"Aye, that band you like… Punk Floyd, said you'd probably want it."

"Pink."

"Pink what?"

"Pink Floyd, the band."

"Sure how would I know what it was. He has it sellotaped up to your wall now so he has it all ready for you."

"Can you tell him I called?"

"Sure can't you tell him yourself. He'll be back here any minute now I'm sure."

"Maybe you tell him. Tell him I was asking for him. I really better go here."

"Go, go surely, must be costin' you a fortune in coins. Save your pennies. You'll give us a wee call again next week?"

"I will."

"Next week."

"Next week… I have to go, coins running out."

"Alright, watch yourself now, and don't forget to say your prayers every night."

"I'll say them."
"And go to mass on Sunday…"
"Mum, I have to go."
"Alright then, Nial."
"Bye bye, Mum."
"Bye bye now, pet. Bye bye."
"Bye."

Nial slammed the phone back onto the hook. He turned quickly and made his way into the train station and down the escalator. He felt dizzy. He braced himself against a wall and began to wretch. It was last night's beer. The greasy canteen breakfast. The worry in his mother's voice. Anderson, and London and England — and more than anything, the thought of his father buying him a Pink Floyd poster… the thought of his father missing him so much he would do such a thing… more than anything, it was that.

As he made his way back to North London on the Tube, Nial stared at his own ghostly reflection in the darkness of the window opposite his seat. A couple of young English lads about the same age as himself got on at Saint John's Wood. They were wearing football scarves and jerseys, chatting loudly about a match they were off to see. Nial found himself full of rage. It took everything he had not to leap up and punch one of them in the mouth. But why? These two lads were just on their way to a football match. Their existence had no bearing on him whatsoever. *These two lads are not your enemy,* he thought. *If they are, they don't even know it.* Nial was picturing them in British Army fatigues, the green camouflage, the black ankle boots, the black beret, the hunter green SA80. It suddenly occurred to him that they might even be Irish. There were lots of Irish lads who came over here for the work and wound up staying in London. Their kids would have English accents. *These two Cockneys could be Paddies* he thought. How many times had he encountered a second generation Irishman in a British army outfit in the North, he wondered?

As the train pulled into Kilburn he caught the eyes of the red-haired boy, some part of them, centuries old, recognized one another. They both turned away immediately. The boys exited the train and as it began to pull away, Nial spotted the red headed boy sneering at him through the window from the platform, two fingers raised in a fuck-you V.

Twenty minutes later he was back in Neasdon.

As he walked by the scrap-metal yards on his way back from the station, he found himself searching for a glimpse of Marissa. He hadn't been able to shake the thought of her for more than a few minutes since he'd last seen her. He felt a hand on his shoulder and he jumped. He turned, and there she was, laughing.

"Sorry, didn't mean to scare you." He almost didn't recognize her at first. She was wearing a dark blue blazer and a matching knee-length skirt which hugged her thighs. Her hair was tied back neatly in a ponytail. It was the first time he'd seen her wearing makeup. The smile was exactly the same. She was stunning. "You're in deep thought," she said, grinning. "You just walked right by me back there."

"Did I? I was just thinking."

"So I see."

"You on your way home?" said Nial.

"At last. I hate working Saturdays."

"Me too." Nial suddenly felt self-conscious of his dusty clothes. His muddy work boots. He looked a mess standing next to her.

"It kills the spirit of the weekend," she continued.

"Aye. I suppose it does."

"What are you so down about?" she said, doing that thing again where she cocked her head sideways to look at him. "Some girl break your heart?"

"No. I just got off the phone with my mother."

"Ah."

"She told me my father bought a 'Punk Floyd' poster for my bedroom wall yesterday."

"Ah… the Punk Floyd. He's expecting you back again soon then?"

"It looks like it."

"Anybody else expecting you back there soon… a wee girl maybe?" She nudged him playfully with her shoulder.

"No. No girl."

"Big family?"

"Just the three of us."

"Tough being an only child sometimes, right? My parents still think I'm ten."

Nail wanted so badly to tell her about Cathal. But she already knew too much. Even this, this innocent banter was too much. They were standing at the intersection of Church Road waiting for the light.

CHURCH END

"You want to go to The White Horse for a beer? My treat," she asked, turning to face him. He felt a tightness in his chest. Her gaze destroyed him.

"Won't Decco be waiting for you?"

"Why would Decco be waiting for me?"

"I thought he was your boyfriend."

"Decco? Would you get away outta that." She tipped her head back and laughed. "He's my flat mate. I barely ever see him, and when I do he's usually wasted. Come on, let me buy you a beer. You must be thirsty after all that hard manly man work."

Three hours later they were still in The White Horse. They had commandeered the two big orange armchairs by the open fire and they hadn't stopped talking other than to buy drinks and use the restroom. Marissa, he discovered, had backpacked alone all through Europe. She'd never had a steady boyfriend. She listened to Blondie, Men at Work, and Tom Waits. She liked London but only as a stepping stone. She was bound for New York as soon as she got the money together. She was an independent spirit… she liked being alone… a lot.

Around them the bar grew busy. It was the usual Saturday evening crowd. A band called Shanty Dam had set up in the corner and were covering everyone from Thin Lizzy to U2. Marty was scuttling back and forth spitting curse words at anybody bold enough to order a drink. The light of the fire danced in the corner of Marissa's eyes, and Nial was so close now he could feel her breath on the side of his face as she talked.

"Oh," she said. "I just remembered. Paul Brady is

playing The Mean Fiddler tonight. We have to go."

"Who's going?"

"Me and you."

"Let's go."

"Do you mind if we stop at the house?" she said as an afterthought. "I really need to get out of this suit."

They drained the last of their drinks and Nial held the door for her as they exited the bar onto Church Road. The night was mild and full of hope. The first real night of summer. A crescent moon lay casually on its back in the dark sky over Wembley. The leaves of the trees whispered as a light breeze carried seeds of doubt and fear tumbling down the street toward Wilsden. The back of Nial's hand brushed against Marissa's and a jolt of electricity passed between them. A fantastic fizzle of energy that danced over his skin and up into the hair on the back of his head. He had just about mustered up the courage to take her hand when he spotted The Baz lurching toward them out of the shadows. His head was drooped and he didn't seem to notice them at all. He was almost gone right past when Nial spoke.

"Hey, Baz. Where are you off to?"

The Baz paused and turned his head back to them. He nodded, slowly smiling at something far away.

"Are you okay?" Nial asked him.

"Yeah, man." The Baz smiled, making a great effort to lift his head to squint at Nial. "Yeah." Marissa's face seemed to register with him too and he turned and slowly continued on his way. Nial called after him.

"Baz. Baz." But he wasn't stopping. He raised his

hand weakly as if he were waving goodbye and went on toward The White Horse.

"You think he's okay?" Nial asked Marissa.

"Nope."

"He doesn't look good."

"He's into some heavy shit lately I've heard."

"What shit?"

"I don't know, it's just rumors."

"What rumors?"

"Smack."

"Heroin? No way… he'd never do that shit."

"There's rumors going round the estate, that's all I'm saying. Squats being broke into when the lads aren't home. Stereos going missing. Decco's bike disappeared a few days ago… Maybe it's not all him, but some of it is."

"Shit. They wouldn't hurt him, would they?"

"I don't know. I'm just telling you because you're close to him. Just be careful being around him, okay."

Marissa leaned in and gave Nial a quick kiss on the cheek. Then she took his hand in hers and she led him in silence toward the estate.

Chapter 10

"Stay close," Marissa said, taking Nial's hand in hers and leading him down the alleyway, past the long queue of people waiting to get into The Mean Fiddler to see Paul Brady.

He didn't need to be dragged. He would have followed her anywhere.

Some lad wolf-whistled as Marissa sailed by in her skin-tight black leather pants. Nial turned to catch him staring at her ass. He felt his fist clench; she felt it too and gave his hand a little pump in hers, a signal to just let it go. She never even paused to look around. She was accustomed to the attention it seemed. He was not.

"Hi Vince," she said to the big-shouldered man stationed at the door. "Room for two more?"

"Decco and the lads are upstairs by the bar," he said, as he lifted the rope and let them sail on in.

"Thanks, babe."

Vince cracked the faintest glimmer of a boyish smile. No one was immune to Marissa's charm it seemed.

CHURCH END

As they headed up the stairs, Marissa explained to Nial that Vince owned the place. He loved the Church End Irish Crew. They were his biggest spenders.

As they reached the upper balcony, Paul Brady was just beginning the first bars of "The Homes of Donegal," one of Nial's favorites. Decco was in a booth over in the corner with a bunch of the Church End crew. Nial recognized all of them: Dublin Paul, Shea Veigh, Johnny The Bulber, Stonewall, and Sad Sue. Terry was passed out in the corner, his head propped against the wall. The smell of hash was thick in the air and Decco was in the process of skinning another joint in his lap. Stonewall stood up and grabbed Sad Sue by the hand, yanking her on to her feet making room for Marissa and Nial to take a seat.

"Come on," Nial heard him say to Sue. "Let's go find Morrison and get him stoned."

"Morrison?" Nial asked.

"Van, he's downstairs somewhere, three sheets to the wind."

"Van Morrison's here?" Nial blurted.

"First time in The Fiddler?" Decco smiled, running his tongue along the glue edge of the spliff.

"Leave him alone," Marissa said, draping her arm over Nial's shoulder and pulling him close. "He's with me."

Nial was relieved to see Decco crack a wide grin. He seemed genuinely pleased to see them together.

Shea Veigh shook a little white powder onto the back of his hand and held it under Terry's nose.

"Watch this," he said. "Yo, Tel, sniff."

Terry, still appearing to be in a deep sleep, took a deep sniff through his nose. The powder disappeared and his eyes popped open. "What?" he said, startled.

"Nothing," Shea said, winking across the table at Nial. "I just thought you'd dozed off there for a second."

"I'm not sleeping."

"No worries. Just checking."

Terry was wide awake again, tapping his hand on the table to the music, his eyes wide and wild. He reached for a beer and took a deep swallow. He was back in the game.

Nial stopped a waitress and ordered drinks for Marissa and himself. She had taken his hand in hers under the table and laid her head on his shoulder.

Decco handed Nial the joint. Nial took it and inhaled deeply.

"You're all right, Tyrone," Decco said, nodding, a wide, sleepy hash grin on his face. Nial smiled right back. It felt good to be part of this crew.

Marissa took a hit and passed the joint on to Terry. She nudged Nial out of the booth and led him to the rail overlooking the stage so they could be alone. The place was jam packed. The crowd on the floor below was shoulder to shoulder, swaying the rhythm of the music. Paul Brady was rocking them peacefully in the palm of his hand. Marissa rested her head on Nial's shoulder and he slipped his arm around her waist. He felt his heart swell and hum until it ached. Marissa must have felt it too for she looked up at him just then with the saddest smile, and he kissed her as she wrapped her arms tightly around him. They embraced each other then and the room seemed to fall away... everything but the warmth of her body and the feel of her lips and the music rising into the ethereal night.

"You can come in," Marissa said. "I promise not to bite." She was dropping the needle on a record. Nial was standing in the doorway of her bedroom, half in, half out.

Now that they were back in her flat, he could see that this was all wrong. The walk back to from The Mean Fiddler had sobered him enough to see that he was digging himself further and further into a hole here. He was lying to her. She didn't even know his real name. He tried to will himself to come clean, but the words refused to come out.

"Who's this?" he managed to say instead.

"Jackson Browne, *Late for the Sky*," she said, holding up the album cover so he could see it. "I love this album."

Marissa's place was the tidiest flat he'd been in since arriving in London. There were curtains on the windows, an actual bedframe and matching chest of drawers, a bedside table with a lamp, a framed poster of a foggy New York City hung on the wall above her bed. Nial crossed to the bedside table and picked up the book she was reading. He opened it to where she had left off, sat, and began reading.

"The taxi went up the hill, passed the lighted square, then on into the dark, still climbing, then leveled out onto a dark street, behind St.-Etienne-du-Mont, went smoothly down the asphalt, passed the trees and the standing bus at the Place de la Contrescarpe…." He looked up to see Marissa unbuttoning her top.

"Don't stop," she said as she draped the black shirt over the back of a chair by the window and turning from him unsnapped her bra. "Keep reading."

He looked back down at the book he held in his hands but he could no longer read. He felt a deep sense of shame. This was wrong. He was an imposter. He swallowed hard.

"Marissa…" he started.

"You don't have to say anything," she said, coming to him and kissing the top of his head and holding him to her. Her skin was as soft and pure as fresh petals. She eased him back down onto the bed and hovered over him, kissing his cheeks, his neck, his chest.

"Stop," he said.

"It's okay, relax."

"No," he said placing his hands gently on her shoulders, "I have to go. I can't stay."

She lifted her head, her brow furrowed. "What do you mean you can't stay?"

As gently as he could, he eased himself out from underneath her.

"What's wrong?" she said. She sounded suddenly like a small child. He could see she was hurt, confused. She lifted the blanket and self-consciously held it over her chest as he stood and walked toward the door.

"I just can't stay, that's all. I'm really sorry."

"I don't get it."

"I'm sorry," he said, and he hurried out of the room,

CHURCH END

down the stairs, out into the night. London was cold again; concrete, wrought iron fences, faded brick, a dog barking, the distant growl of a midnight bus climbing Church Road toward the police station.

Chapter 11

"Hi. You. Tyrone. Get over here." Nial looked up from the hinge plate he was chopping on an oak door. Dessie. It was a week since he'd seen Dessie in his office. He'd almost given up hope that anything would come of their little chat.

Dessie gave him a nod to follow him outside. The Burner gave Nial a puzzled glance. Dessie wasn't accustomed to showing up on the site to just shoot the breeze. Nial set the hammer and chisel aside and followed Dessie outside into a light rain. Dessie pulled an envelope from his inside jacket pocket and handed it to Nial. Nial reached for it, but Dessie held onto it, forcing Nial to lift his head and make eye contact.

"I'll be seeing you around, Pat," he said. Another line had been crossed. He watched Dessie stride back across the mucky worksite toward a black Mercedes parked in the street. Dessie was owed now.

Nial ripped open the envelope and inside was a single

piece of white paper with a handwritten address on it:

15 Wood Lane
Shepherds Bush.

There it was. Anderson's address. He had it. He wanted to go right away. See the place. See if it was really him. Nial had only ever seen Anderson in pictures. *An Phoblacht* had published a couple of grainy photographs of him after the court case. Cathal's death and the subsequent trial had been well documented in the Republican newspaper. Other stories of Anderson had emerged along the way, stories of him abusing Catholics at checkpoints in the North. He wasn't well liked even in his own regiment. One anonymous source described him as "a sadist, and a sicko who had been itching to kill a Catholic, any Catholic since his first day on the force." Anderson wasn't a soldier, he was a psycho in fatigues, with a gun, and a license to kill.

Nial felt certain that if the IRA had been able to get to him while he was still stationed in the North that they would have eliminated him themselves. But once the trial was over and he was acquitted on the grounds that it was an "accidental discharge," Nial knew he would be off their priority list. Resources would not be wasted trying to track Anderson down in London to terminate him. There were too many others just like Anderson still on patrol in the six counties to worry about.

"What did that clown want?" The Burner asked, when Nial returned to his work.

"They made a mistake with my check last week. It came up short. He just brought me the difference."

"Never knew him to be the generous sort," The Burner said, turning away.

"Maybe he likes me."

"Aye, that must be it," The Burner said, adjusting the blade on his plane a hair and gliding it along the edge of a door, sending a fine thread of maple curling onto the dusty floor.

That evening after work Nial took the train to Shepherd's Bush. The rain had faired and here and there the sun crept through the cracks in the clouds throwing silvery threads of light into the grey evening. The city air felt clean… washed, as he followed the directions on his newly purchased A to Z map of London town.

It took less than ten minutes for Nial to find 15 Wood Lane. He stood at a safe distance across the street to observe the place. To his surprise, it was a small, nondescript electronics repair shop. The window display was a mess of old televisions, radios, VCRs, and toasters.

Nial pulled a cigarette from his pack and absently placed it between his lips. He considered strolling across the street and entering the store but his hands were already trembling. He couldn't risk it. He needed to stay calm, think this through; this was not the time for a dumb, careless move. He'd waited too long for this opportunity. Just then, the shop door opened, and out stepped Anderson. Nial recognized him instantly. He looked exactly as he had in the picture. He hadn't even bothered to shave his handlebar mustache.

Anderson pulled a bunch of keys from his coat pocket and locked the door, giving the handle a firm shake to make sure it was properly bolted. He was a big man. His coat was tight on his broad shoulders. He turned and twirling the keys on his right index finger, he strode off down the street with an air of authority, with the air of a man who was used to having things go his way. Nial followed him.

By the time they reached the end of the street, Nial was no more than five steps behind Anderson. His heart thundered with a violent rage. Here was the man who'd murdered his brother. The man who'd devastated his family. He balled his fist and imagined how it would feel to punch him hard in the side of the head. He wanted so badly to pummel him, pour his hatred into him, pound on his face until he bled, tear him to pieces… If only he'd brought a butcher knife, he could have ended this thing right here on the street, in an instant. He could barely breathe with the pressure built up in his chest.

Anderson stopped to wait for the stoplight to change. He pulled a pack of smokes from his pocket and lit one with a silver Zippo. Nial was standing no more than three feet behind him. Anderson must have sensed the sudden shift in energy. He spun around quickly to face Nial.

"You alright, mate?" he said, in a heavy Cockney accent. Nial stared at him unable to speak. "Oh…" Anderson said taking the lighter out of his pocket again and flicked the flame under the cigarette still hanging from Nial's lips. Nial had forgotten it was still there. He inhaled deeply as Anderson fanned the flame under the tip until it caught, then he flicked the Zippo closed and dropped it back in his jacket pocket.

Without a word, or a nod of acknowledgment for the light, Nial stepped quickly around Anderson, and walked off.

"You're fucking welcome mate," Anderson yelled after him. "Prick."

Nial continued on without turning around. He circled the block and came back to stand across the street from the small store. He was going to need Dessie again for one more favor.

Nial walked back toward the train station and took the Metropolitan line up to Baker Street. Rush hour was long over and the train rocked softly along the tracks. At Paddington station the doors opened and Anderson stepped into the car. He was still swinging the bundle of keys on his index finger, only now he was dressed in full military fatigues and a pair of shining black boots. He grinned at Nial. Nial froze. Anderson stepped quickly toward him pulling a gun from his pocket and leveled it at Nial's head. The train came to an abrupt stop and Nial woke with a start, jumping from his seat. He was alone. The car was empty. He glanced at the station name on the platform wall: Barking. He was at the end of the line. He must have been asleep for well over an hour.

It was almost midnight before he made his way back to Harlesden. The moonlight hit the stacks of scrap metal at Neasdon turning them into surreal mangled space colonies scattered over a lunar landscape. A guard dog bounced himself off the chain-link fence and Nial shuddered against the sudden cold wind that whipped down the neck of his shirt and into the very core of his spine. He buried his hands deep in his pockets for comfort and hurried along toward Church End Estate conjuring images of Marissa curled up in bed reading Hemingway under a soft light. He hadn't seen her in over a week, since he'd walked out of her bedroom without an explanation. When he reached the estate he went out of his way to walk by her place, but all the windows were in darkness. He stood for a moment staring up at the sky. If God had bothered to look down, right then, he'd have witnessed the pale face of a young Irish boy, standing alone on a dark planet, staring up at the sky with eyes glistening like tiny stars.

At nine the next morning Nial was back in Shepherd's Bush standing directly across the street from the little repair shop. He had decided to forgo work for the day. He had come to London to avenge the death of his brother and that is exactly what he intended to do. He'd come too far now to turn back. He needed to stay focused on the task at hand. He needed to kill Anderson and get out of England as quickly as possible.

He'd spent the whole night twisting and turning in his bed. His thoughts carried him down every twisted tunnel imaginable. Was he really capable of taking a man's life? Would God banish his soul into eternal darkness if he committed murder? Was Marissa spending the night in someone else's bed? Was God trying to save him from darkening his soul by putting Marissa directly in his path? He wanted so desperately to give up and go home. But when he woke in a mess of sheets to the screeching brakes of a double decker bus on Church Road, he still wanted Anderson dead.

By the time he had arrived, the small store was already open. He couldn't see Anderson in there past the mess in the dark window, but the sign had been turned on the door to read Open. And inside, a light had been switched on.

He pictured Anderson back there at work under a bench light tinkering with the innards of an old radio. There was no way he could risk going in there to look around and size the place up. He'd already raised Anderson's antenna once by taking a light from him. Anderson would suspect trouble immediately if he saw him again.

Just to be safe he'd worn a different jacket this morning and a black wool hat that he pulled down to the bridge of his nose so that Anderson wouldn't recognize him. To avoid suspicion he took care to keep moving. He circled the block, strolling casually, avoiding eye contact with strangers, and kept a copy of the A to Z London guidebook in his hand in case he was questioned by a curious Bobby... He could always play the dumb tourist.

At exactly ten o'clock Anderson left the shop, walked three blocks to buy a breakfast sandwich, and picked up a copy of *The Sun*. He was back in the repair shop within twenty minutes. At eleven, the mailman arrived with a few small packages and a couple of envelopes. No one else entered the store before noon. Nial had seen enough. He knew what had to be done.

Nial was back on the site at Kings Cross at one p.m. just as the men were returning from their lunch break. The Burner was already back at work ahead of the rest. He was assembling a stud wall on the floor before erecting it. Nial noticed that his own tool belt lay on the floor beside where The Burner was working.

"Good afternoon, stranger," The Burner said, dryly, as Nial approached and lifted his tool belt to strap it on.

"Did the foreman come by?" Nial asked.

"He did."

"Do I still have a job?"

"I told him you'd just stepped out to the John. He's none the wiser."

"Thank you."

"Yer welcome. Now maybe you could lend me a hand. Grab the other side of this wall and help me stand it up."

Nial appreciated The Burner not digging around for details. He was a good man.

Nial grabbed one side of the stud wall and between The Burner and himself, they stood it up and tapped it into position. It fit snug as a glove. There was so much comfort in working with a master carpenter. Maybe when this was all over and done with, Nial thought, he'd devote himself to the trade more fully. Become something valuable in the world.

Nial had decided that the best way to get rid of Anderson was to blow up the repair shop, with Anderson in it. He would need to stay close to the store to make sure no innocent bystanders got caught up in the explosion. He'd weighed his options and a bomb seemed like the most foolproof one. Anderson was too big for him to tackle head on. He was a formidable character. He wouldn't go down easily. Stabbing or shooting was completely out of the question. The risk of failure was way too high. Besides, Nial wasn't sure he had it in him to stick a knife into another human. A bomb was easier… less personal. He understood now why the bomb was the preferred method of the IRA back home. It made a difference when you didn't have to see a man's eyes up close when he died. A bomb depersonalized the situation… a child could push a button on a detonator.

Dessie had told Nial that if he needed anything, that he could get it. Nial was going to need a bomb. One small enough to send through the mail in a small package. Given the nature of Anderson's business, it shouldn't be very difficult to get an explosive device into his hands.

After work, Nial made his way to McGinley's office to see Dessie one more time.

CHURCH END

"Well, if it isn't my little hippie friend." Dessie grinned as Nial came through the door of his office. Nial could tell Dessie was delighted to have him back... delighted to have him indebted. Dessie leaned back in his seat, put his shoes up on his desk and knitted his meaty fingers behind his meaty head. "How'd that address work out for you?"

"Great. Thank you for that," Nial said.

"Oh you're quite welcome. No bother at all. You found your man, did you?"

"I did."

"Ach, isn't that lovely. Did you stop in to say hello to him, did you?"

"Not yet."

"Oh?"

"I have another favor to ask?"

"Oh you do, do you!" Dessie said dropping his shoes off the edge of the table and leaning forward. His hair looked particularly greasy today, even his skin had an oily sheen to it, like he'd bathed in a chipper.

"I'll pay," Nial offered weakly.

"Fucken right big spender we have over here, eh." Dessie poked. "You're not drinking all your money away down The White Horse then?"

Nial didn't like the way he'd referred to The White Horse. Yes, he'd mentioned the place to Dessie when he'd first met him, but it was a strange thing to bring up out of the blue... Was he telling him that he was being watched?

"I need a bomb."

"Oh, be jasus! A bomb, he says. And you think old

Dessie can get you something like that, do you?"

"I do."

"What about your little Dublin buddy?" Dessie said, shifting gears. "You seen him around lately?"

"No..." Nial said, but he realized suddenly that Dessie was toying with him. Of course, if he knew how to find Anderson, he could find The Baz in his sleep. "I might have bumped into him once or twice in The White Horse."

"Ah," Dessie said. "So you have seen him."

"Yes."

"Well you happen to see that slippy little junky cunt again, can you please tell him that I'd like him to come see old Dessie when he has a break in his hectic schedule."

"I will."

"Good lad, good lad." Dessie lifted a pencil off the desk and started picking his teeth with it. Nial was tempted to tell him that he was scribbling lead all over his front teeth, but he decided to let it slide. "What sort of a... device... were you in the market for?"

"Something small, small enough to fit in a package. I'm going to mail it to him. Powerful enough to take him out, but not destroy the whole building."

"Something about the size of a block of butter then?"

"I suppose so, yes."

"... or a dead squirrel."

Nial laughed awkwardly. But Dessie wasn't laughing.

"Your hands are getting dirtier, boy," Dessie said, fixing him with a stare that made Nial's blood run cold.

"You ready to get dirty... boy?"

"That's what I need."

"Alright then. You shall have it."

"How much?" Nial asked.

"Oh, we'll figure out a price later."

"I'd rather know now if you don't mind."

"Oh, but I do mind," Dessie said, and he smiled, a wide lead-stained smile that made the hair on Nial's arms stand on end.

Chapter 12

Nial woke bleary-eyed to a heavy banging on the door. He was disoriented. The house was dark, apart from the orange glow of the streetlight awash on the living room walls. Nial had fallen asleep sitting upright in the armchair after coming back from meeting Dessie at his office.

Before he could muster the clarity to rise from his seat, the banging had started again. It sounded angry. Maybe the cops had tracked them down over the stolen mattress. He stood for a moment longer hoping that whoever it was would give up and go away. But the banging continued. Maybe it was The Baz, maybe he'd gotten stoned and locked himself out.

He rose and made his way toward the front door. Through the frosted glass he could make out the silhouette of a short man.

"Who is it?" Nial said, reflexively squeezing his back tight against the wall in the dark corridor in case a shot was fired through the door in his general direction.

"Pat. Is that you?" Marissa. He pulled open the door and there she was, more beautiful than ever, wearing a black leather biker jacket, white t-shirt, and a pair of faded jeans, her hair pulled back in a ponytail that hung over her left shoulder. Before he could say anything she had stepped forward and slipped her arms around his waist, and she was kissing him, with a mouth that tasted like wine and honey. He closed the door behind her and they made their way, stumbling, into the front room, and onto his mattress without another word.

Afterwards, she laid her head on his chest and they lay for a moment bathed in a perfect silence and the orange glow of the streetlamp that flooded the room.

"You disappeared on me," she said, breaking the spell.

She must have sensed him tense.

"What are you hiding from Pat? Don't you trust me yet?" She lifted her head to look into his eyes. She was searching for something. She had a way of seeing into him that made him want to lay it all on the table.

There was a noise at the door. A key. Fumbling. It opened, and they listened in silence as The Baz staggered into the hallway and stumbled his way into the kitchen. Then he knocked into the table and a chair and things went quiet again.

"I should go check on him. Just to make sure he's okay." Nial said as he slipped on his jeans and softly made his way down the hallway to the kitchen door.

The Baz was sitting at the kitchen table. His sleeve

was rolled up past his elbow and he was wrapping a rubber band around his upper arm. The needle and spoon sat on the table in front of him next to that a small plastic bag of brown powder. He looked up at Nial, but his eyes were already dead. There was no startled reaction. No rush to change course. He was already numb to the world.

"Jesus Baz, what the fuck are you doing?"

"What the fuck do you care?" His voice was low and foreign.

"I care. Don't put that shit in your arm, man, you'll kill yourself."

"Chill man, chill." The Baz lifted the spoon and the bag and continued with his fix. "It's my fucken arm. You, fuck off."

Nial felt stung. He was tempted to grab the needle and bag and fling them into the bin, slap Baz around a bit, but instead he closed the kitchen door softly, and walked back to his own room. Back to Marissa.

He sat on the end of the mattress with his back to her and lit a cigarette.

"What happened?" She whispered.

"You were right. He's using."

Marissa pulled the sheet about her and slipped her legs around Nial's waist.

"I think he's in love with you," she said. Nial tried to move away from her, but she held on to him.

"What the fuck, Marissa!"

"It never occurred to you?"

"No, it didn't fucking occur to me."

"It was the first thing I thought when I saw you two

together, that first night I met you."

"You thought I was gay?"

"No, I thought he'd finally found someone he really liked… I couldn't figure you out at all… I still can't."

"The Baz is gay?"

"Have you ever seen him with a girl?"

Nial felt like an idiot. How could he not have known? The Baz had practically spelled it out for him again and again… The Baz was not interested in women like that.

"Fuck. Am I an idiot, or what?"

"No. You didn't know. Now you do."

"Fuck." Nial put his head in his hands. This had gotten way more complicated than it should have: The Baz, Marissa, Dessie, the whole Irish crew in the housing estate… even The Burner. He was becoming enmeshed in a life here in London that he'd never intended, and no one, not one person, even knew his name.

"I think I need to go for a long walk," he said, finally.

"I'll come with you, if you like," Marissa offered.

"No. I think I need to be alone right now."

Marissa released him from her embrace. She got out of the bed, dressed quickly, and left without another word. Nial watched her leave and then dropped back onto the mattress and stared at the ceiling for an eternity. He should never have allowed her into his bed. He should never have agreed to share a squat with The Baz. He should have stayed alone. The house was silent. He listened for any movement in the kitchen. Nothing.

When he opened the kitchen door Baz was still sitting where he had left him, his head rolled over to one side, unconscious. The used needle was on the table. A blue-black bruise in the cup of his arm with a tiny red pin prick at the heart of it.

Nial checked to make sure he was breathing, bundled a jacket and propped it under his head so his neck didn't cramp, and left him there to sleep it off. He really did need to go for a long walk.

Outside a sharp wind seemed to curl in at him from every direction. Every which way he twisted his head he was still facing the breeze. He walked up through Harlesden, past the police station, The Mean Fiddler, and the Jubilee Clock. He wanted to get as far away from anyone who might recognize him as possible. He walked into an old pub called The Green Man. There were only a handful of people inside at the bar. An English crowd. A few heads turned his way but they passed him little mind. He took a stool and ordered a beer and sat in silence. There was no radio playing in the background. No jukebox blaring in the corner. Hushed conversations were taking place around the bar. A soft chuckle here. A head nodding in agreement there. A finger raised politely for another beer. The customers were mostly older men, maybe twenty or so of them. Nial found great comfort in the civility of it all. Was this Jolly Old England? Or was this an oasis, beyond all that nonsense, beyond time or country? Whatever it was it felt good, he decided. He was one Catholic lad in a room full of English men and he felt entirely at ease… and safe.

By his third beer he had the urge to run out of the bar and not stop sprinting until he was back in Marissa's arms. He wanted to apologize to her. Tell her his real name. Tell her everything... the truth... Cathal, Anderson, Dessie, all of it... but that would be madness. What if she told someone else? Who's to say she wouldn't go straight to the cops? Dessie would have him killed if he opened his mouth. The cops would throw him jail in a heartbeat. He thought about The Baz. The first real friend he'd had in a long time. The Baz had taken him in, gotten him hooked up with his first job, introduced him to Marissa. He'd even stole a bed for him so he'd have somewhere comfortable to sleep on his first night. What good was avenging Cathal's death if he wound up hurting so many other good people in the process?

Nial got the attention of the bartender and ordered a double vodka. The bartender eyed him with some concern, as if to say, *Please don't be that Irish lad in here.* Nial took the drink and downed it in one, sliding the glass back across the bar for a refill before the bartender could even walk away. It was going to take a lot of vodka to make the world right again.

Chapter 13

The following week passed without much fanfare. Nial stayed away from The White Horse to avoid running into Marissa. He had made a silent commitment to his dead brother and to his family to serve justice, and no emotional entanglement was going to stand in the way of that.

Every night after work he walked to a pub outside of the immediate area to avoid bumping into anyone he knew from Church End Estate. One night he went to Biddy Mulligan's in Kilburn, another, The Spotted Dog in Wilsden. Saturday night he walked all the way to The National in Kilburn. The place was crammed wall to wall with Irish immigrants like himself there to see an Irish band called Intuanua.

Nial got a drink at the upstairs bar and made his way to the balcony overlooking the dance floor and stage. To his amazement he found himself standing shoulder to shoulder with Elvis Costello and Shane

CHURCH END

MacGowan. The two singers were having a pint and a chat, watching the band perform, and no one seemed to have the slightest clue as to who they were. They fit right in with this band of ruffians.

Nial was no sooner standing next to them at the railing until a vicious fight broke out on the dance floor below. At first MacGowan and Costello were laughing along at the madness. As the fight began to spread throughout the whole place, it had a domino effect, bodies bumping into other bodies from a central point, until a thousand fists started swinging at once. A chair was launched from the sidelines. Within seconds it had spread upstairs to the balcony like a wild brushfire, and before there was even time to consider an exit, someone had cold-cocked Nial and he found himself sprawled on the floor with MacGowan on top of him, scrambling for cover. Beer bottles were being smashed, women were screaming, bodies were hurtling into one another; something primitive had been unleashed... a wild, crimson rage.

Nial managed to get to his feet and made a dash for the main door. He'd had enough entertainment for one Saturday night. Outside he got lucky and found a cab right away. When they got up to Harlesden, the Pakistani cab driver refused to drive into the estate for fear of his life, so Nial got out on Church Road to walk the rest of the way home.

He was angry with the driver. He had hoped for a clean passage to his own front door. But once he was out of the car and walking through the darkened alleyways of the estate he felt helpless against the magnetic pull of Marissa's embrace. The alcohol and loneliness had weakened his resolve. He stood for a long while staring up at her bedroom window in a trance, torn between his sense of duty to his dead brother and the slim glimmer of hope that she might miraculously appear and invite him inside. He hadn't even noticed that the rain had begun until he felt water streaming down his face. He was soaked through. The cool rain sobered him into acceptance. There would be no bedroom light to save him tonight. He shivered against the cold and made his way home to bed, alone.

It rained for the next four days straight.

The entire worksite at Kings Cross was a mess of puddles and muck. By Thursday Nial was so sick of it all he almost threw in the towel to head for the airport. He'd even managed to upset The Burner in his effort to keep everyone at arm's length. He was at his wit's end. The never-ending series of hangovers, the lying, and the loneliness, left him feeling half cracked. He had begun to accept that it was over, he had lost something in himself, something was missing. He would go home to Tyrone to see if he could retrieve it, become whole again, leave Anderson's fate for God's final judgement.

That's when Dessie arrived with the news.

Nial hung back and watched him hand out the checks to the lads as he always did on a Thursday. Then when he stepped up to get his own, Dessie said, "Follow me, you little prick."

Nial followed him without a word back to his black Mercedes across the parking lot and got in. Dessie sat for a moment looking around to make sure they were not being watched, but no one could possibly see through the rain as it thundered on the roof and ran in sheets down the windows.

Dessie reached into his jacket pocket and produced another envelope.

"All the information on where to pick up that thing is inside here. Don't you fucken screw this up. This is happening as a favor to me and I don't need any shit coming back my way. You so much as breathe my name in connection to any of this and I'll kill you. Understand?"

"Got it." Nial reflexively gave Dessie a sharp military salute. Without pause Dessie slapped him hard in the face and locked his hands around Nial's throat.

"You think this is a fucken joke, you little cunt?" Dessie put his nose right up to Nial's face and locked his eyes on him. "You have any idea how fucking deep you're in here?"

Nial got it. It had been a dumb thing to do.

"I'm sorry. I didn't mean to disrespect you. I'm sorry, Dessie."

Dessie's breathing was heavy and labored as he searched Nial's eyes for any hint of betrayal, then he released him.

"Go. Get the fuck out of my car. And remember: you fuck this up and I'll hang you up by your feet and skin you like a rabbit."

Nial got out, shoved the envelope into his pocket, and hopped his way over a series of mucky puddles on his way back toward the main building.

In an empty room on the fourth floor he removed the envelope from his pocket and ripped it open. His hands were shaking from the violence of Dessie's threat.

This is how things escalated as you moved toward the act of murder, he thought. Was this God's way of telling him to turn back? Was this too a sign? *Do not go beyond this point.* Could he actually wind up on a hook, Dessie starting in on him with a knife? He shuddered at the thought. Of course he could. Such things happened in the world to men who continued to press on beyond the warning signs. He forced the line of thinking from his head, disregarded it as unwarranted paranoia and fear, and he focused on the envelope.

Inside was a scrap of paper with an address and a time.

Nial read the information in a low whisper:

Stand in front of Chi Chi's Mexican restaurant on Leicester Square at four thirty pm Friday. Have one thousand pounds cash in a brown envelope in your hand.

Jesus, Friday! That was tomorrow. He wasn't sure quite what he had expected. But it seemed too sudden. This was it. Someone had been tasked with building him an explosive device, an actual bomb, and now he was going to have to take it in his own hands on a crowded city street outside a popular tourist restaurant in the middle of rush hour.

There was no way out. He lit a cigarette and inhaled deeply. He would have to be there. This would be his only chance. Maybe he could get the bomb into the mail tomorrow night. This was it. He shoved the envelope back in his pocket, then he opened the envelope that held his check. This would be the last McGinley's check he would ever receive as Pat Coyle. Next week he could start putting everything back to normal again. No more hiding. No more lying. No more Pat Coyle, no more Dessie, or The Baz, or The Burner… or Marissa. He would forget her eventually. He just had to get out of London. He just had to get as far away from all of it as humanly possible.

It had been almost a week since he'd seen her, but there wasn't a minute that went by that he didn't think of her. It would be different once he got back to Tyrone, he told himself. He would force himself to forget her. He just had to.

On his way back downstairs Nial caught The Burner standing alone by a half-open window watching an old man dig a hole in the rain. Nial joined him for a chat. What the hell! It didn't matter now. He was leaving London in less than a week anyway.

"Poor bastard, doesn't understand he has a choice," The Burner said as they stared down at the drenched man in a mess of wet blue clay.

"Maybe he needs the beer money."

"Wants… the beer money. Not needs."

"Maybe he feels like he needs it."

"Can you imagine any beer that would be worth that level of degradation?"

"Maybe he enjoys digging holes in the rain. Maybe that's his thing," Nial said. The Burner chuckled a little at that one.

"Maybe you're right," he said. "Maybe you're right." Just then Harry the foreman suddenly stormed out of the canteen and, pulling his jacket up over his head to shield himself from the torrential downpour, ran over to the old man, and began pointing and yelling at him. They couldn't make out the words, but you didn't need to hear what was being said; an old Irishman was down in a blue clay hole with a spade getting rained on as an English foreman screamed at him. That was all the translation needed for this particular situation.

"I'd like to cave that man's head in with a hammer," The Burner said softly.

Nial spotted a half bag of cement sitting in the corner of the room. He hurried over and with considerable effort hoisted it into his arms. He stepped back over to the half open window as The Burner watched him with a bemused sense of curiosity. Harry was about fifteen feet away and moving toward the main entrance to the building directly below them.

"That's a heavy bag of cement you have there. Want to watch it doesn't fall out a window and hurt somebody," The Burner said calmly.

Nial dropped the bag at the last second. It fell the two floors and there was a loud thud. Like the sound of a half bag of cement landing on a man's head. Harry crumpled to the ground in a cloud of fine green dust. He was motionless.

The old man with the spade looked up and saw Nial and The Burner there at the window. The Burner raised his finger to his lips. The old boy gave them a toothy grin and a thumbs up. He scurried out of the hole, flung the spade into the mud, and made his way toward the canteen for some warm lunch.

"I think you and I should look busy for the next couple of hours, Mr. Coyle. There are going to be a lot of people asking questions around here very shortly," The Burner said, dropping the last of his cigarette out the window onto the foreman.

"Do you think I killed him?" Nial asked as they made their way out of the room.

"No such luck. A fiver says it's a concussion."

"You're on."

They shook on it.

It was about an hour later before two police officers approached Nial and The Burner.

"We'd like to ask you gents a few questions if you don't mind," the officer began. He was a young cop, no more than twenty-three or -four, with a healthy pink glow about his cheeks and a thin, weak mustache.

"Fire away," The Burner said, shaking a couple of cigarettes out of his pack for himself and Nial. "We could use a smoke break. Couldn't we, Pat?"

"Right," the cop started. "Have either of you any knowledge of the incident that took place just outside here about an hour ago?"

"Incident?" The Burner asked in his slow deliberate drawl. "Pray tell."

"Approximately one hour ago someone dropped a bag of Portland cement out of a window on this side of the building, seriously injuring a site foreman."

"No! By God that sounds like something I'd remember alright," The Burner answered calmly. "Is he alright, this foreman fellow?"

"He's been taken down to the hospital in an ambulance with a pretty nasty concussion and a broken collar bone."

"What on earth is the world coming to, Officer..." The Burner said, placing a comforting hand on the young cop's shoulder. "...when a man can't go about his day's work without some yobo dropping a bag of cement on his head? What kind of a Godforsaken town is this anyway?"

"It's certainly unfortunate."

"And the foreman," The Burner continued, "the injured party... Did you get his name?"

"Harry..."

"No... not 'our' Harry? Well, for the love of Christ, who would want to hurt that sweet, sweet man?"

"It's hard to comprehend."

"The animals!"

"What about your friend here, did you see anything suspicious that might be of help?"

"Sure wasn't the lad here by my side since breakfast this morning..."

"No, I didn't see anything, Officer."

"Poor sweet Harry... you're sure it was Harry?"

"It was definitely Harry."

"Well, for the love of God!" Burner said blessing himself. "That is a shocker."

"It is. Well, thanks for your help. If you hear anything, you make sure to let me know. We'd like to catch this bastard."

"As would I," Burner said through gritted teeth. "By God I'd like to get my hands on him."

"Well, if you men hear anything… anything at all… you let me know."

"You can count on it, Officer." As the officer turned to walk away The Burner was still shaking his head in complete disgust. Nial thought he noticed a tiny tear in the corner of his eye. Then The Burner turned to him and grinned as he did a little mock jig. "Somebody owes me five pounds."

Nial clapped and laughed; it was the first genuine laugh he'd had in a long while. "Wow. That was some performance."

"Tuam Regional Theatre Company, "60 to 66," The Burner said as he flipped off his imaginary cap and took a wide, theatrical bow.

Chapter 14

"All right, lads… let's get fucken locked," yelled a big, soft-looking lad they called Tomatoes, for his rosy red cheeks, as he flipped his hammer about twenty feet across the room into the gang box with an enormous clatter. Tomatoes was from either Cork or Kerry… one of those counties down the country where their accent was so peculiar Nial had been convinced for the first couple of weeks on the site that it had to be an act.

Tomatoes lived for the porter. He'd drink pints to beat the band. There wasn't a man to match him. Tomatoes drank so much porter he'd developed the rotund countenance of beer barrel. A very happy beer barrel. He was the kind of man who you could see still chortling on a barstool at ninety. He was an easy lad to like… and Tomatoes lived for Thursday evenings… most of the lads did. It was why they worked so hard all week.

Thursday evenings all the lads from the worksite

CHURCH END

went to the pub across the street. The Red Lion was where they got their paychecks cashed. Most of these men did not have bank accounts. Many of them, like Nial, were operating under assumed names. Some were on the run. Others, in hiding, from the law, family, or ex-wives. Every one of these men drank. It was great business for a bar like The Red Lion. There was very little risk involved in cashing a check watermarked "McGinley's." Every bar in town knew a McGinley's check was money in the bank. The bartenders collected the checks and passed them into a back room for processing. The mysterious processing situation might take hours. In the meantime, the bar had a crowd of thirsty Irish men held hostage for the night. Using the bar as a banking system was a crude form of commerce, but for most of them it was the only banking system they knew. Many of the men that Nial knew, would liquidize every penny of their check in the Red Lion before payday rolled around again. Most were dodging demons; they willingly took whatever escape they could afford. Most didn't care where the wages went… just so long as the beer didn't run out.

Nial tried to avoid The Red Lion as much as possible. He had heard enough stories of drunk Irish lads getting rolled on their way home with a pocket full of cash to know it was a fool's game. A drunk Paddy with sawdust on his boots on the train on a Thursday night may as well hang a placard around his neck reading: Mug Me.

Nial headed back, north, toward The White Horse. Marty would cash his check later. He needed this money. Every penny.

As he walked past the scrap-metal yards in Neasdon that evening, he bunched his shoulders helplessly against the rain. He looked for Marissa in the windows of the shabby offices along the street. He ached at the thought of her. Is this what love felt like? He had little experience in this arena. Sure he'd had a crush on a girl or two in high school but nothing had ever made him ache like this. No girl had ever made him want to weep in her absence. As he walked he gave in to a few tears. There was so much rain streaming down his face not even he was sure if he was really crying.

He skipped The White Horse altogether and continued into Church End Estate. He was cold and wet and in no mood for being social. He made his way through a maze of alleyways and dilapidated footpaths: Reade Walk, Taylors Lane. English names. Protestant names. Every syllable felt more oppressive than the last. Who were these Taylors and Reades? What person in their right mind wanted to be honored on a wall plaque in a subsidized housing estate in North London? Maybe the construction workers made up the names as they worked, he thought. Perhaps Nigel Taylor was a brickie. John Reade a carpenter.

The rain stopped suddenly as if someone turned off a spigot. The sun split a crack in the clouds and found his upturned face. Warmth. The estate had been washed clean. It seemed fresher than it should. A light mist softened the grimness of the place, making it feel almost homely for a change. But still, some small, nameless fear tugged at him. Something was wrong. He could feel it. He hurriedly skipped up the stairs to his own landing as if a quick jog might help shake it off.

When he reached the door to his squat, the door was wide open. The wood was splintered around where the lock had been. Someone had kicked it in.

Nial stood on the landing for a second unsure whether he should enter or not. He knew there was little of value in the place. His own cash was hidden under a floorboard in the upstairs bathroom. You'd have to demolish the building to find that stash. But what if he'd disturbed the robbers, what if they were still in there, waiting?

Nial inched his way into the doorway and peered into the dark front hall.

"Hello. Anyone home?"

Nothing.

He glanced around to see if there was something he might be able to brandish as a weapon before going further. Nothing. He dodged into the kitchen, grabbed an empty vodka bottle off the kitchen table, and held it aloft by the neck.

"If you're in here, don't come at me, I've got a knife."

Nothing.

"I'll fucken use it."

The house was deathly silent. He stood for a long while waiting.

Nothing.

"Okay, here I come," he yelled as he rushed down the short hallway into his own room at the front of the house. The mattress was overturned. The television was smashed on its face on the floor. A few records were in vinyl shards against the wall. Books were strewn all over the place. The few pieces of clothing he owned were tossed around carelessly. They'd even torn the Billy Idol poster off the wall.

Nial turned and made his way cautiously up the stairs. He nudged open the bathroom door with his toe and jumped backwards, prepared to strike. The Baz lay fully dressed in the empty tub with a needle hanging out of his arm. A thread of saliva hung from the corner of his mouth.

"Baz," Nial yelled, but there wasn't a budge out of him. "Baz," he shouted again, dropping to his knees and slapping him hard on the face. He was still breathing. But he was far gone. Nial reached for the cold water tap and switched it on full. That got his attention. Baz lifted his arms and struggled weakly but Nial held him in it. "Stay where you are. You have to wake up. Jesus Baz, what the fuck did you do to yourself?" He slapped him again and The Baz groaned lowly, but his eyes started to open a little and he recognized Nial.

"There you are," Nial said. "That's it. It's going to be alright. I got you. You hear me okay?"

The Baz nodded.

"Say it, say yes… I hear you."

"Yes, I hear you… please turn off the water."

"Okay. Come on. Let's get you out of these clothes and into bed."

"I love you," Baz blurted as Nial got an arm around him to hoist him up out of the tub. Nial let it go. But Baz was coming around and he needed Nial to hear it. "I love you, Pat."

"I know, my friend… I know. Come on, let's get you dry, okay?"

"Okay?"

"You love me?"

"Not like that Baz. No, but you're my friend… Okay?"

"Okay," The Baz said, and then he began to whimper softly. "I'm sorry… I'm sorry… I just love you so much. I'm sorry."

"It's okay mate. I got you."

Nial got his arms around Baz and practically carried him to his bedroom across the hallway. He weighed nothing. He was little more than the wet clothes he was wearing.

"You're going to have to eat something soon or there'll be nothing left of you to put a sweater on," Nial said, sitting him on the edge of the bed. Baz tried to lay down on his back but Nial held him up again. "No sleeping yet. I'm going to take your shoes and socks off, and your sweater, but you're going to have to take the rest off yourself… I'm not touching your fucking jocks, okay?"

"Okay." Baz sniffled. Nial was relieved to see Baz manage a weak smile. He was coming back into himself. He would be allright. Nial pulled off his boots and socks and sweater and left him for a moment to sort out the rest. As he closed the bedroom door behind him, he heard The Baz say, "Thank you. I'm sorry."

"Stop saying you're sorry. It's okay." He closed the door behind him.

Nial went back into the bathroom and locked the

door. He pried out the few loose floor tiles in the corner by the sink, and then using a penny, removed the couple of screws that held a short floorboard in place. Once he had the board out of the way, he reached his arm into what looked like a rat hole in the wall underneath the sink… No one in their right mind would slip their hand into that hole no matter how badly they needed a fix. The envelope was still there.

Nial counted his cash. There was just over twelve hundred pounds and he still had today's check to cash. More than enough to take care of Dessie's friend tomorrow at the hand-off and get out of London sometime next week. He would fly to Dublin. Maybe stay in Dublin City for a few weeks. Get a job. Make a little extra cash before heading back North to his family.

Nial slipped the envelope of cash back into the hole, replaced the floorboard and the tiles. He made a big deal of flushing the toilet and running the water in the sink before he returned to check on the Baz.

Baz had fallen asleep. But he'd managed to get out of his wet clothes and under the blankets, his head on a pillow. Nial put his hand on his shoulder and gave him a little shake. Baz opened his eyes and looked up at him.

"You alright?"

"I just need to sleep this off." Baz said.

"You sure?"

"Aye."

"Don't fucken die on me in here."

"I'm sorry. I'm going to get off this stuff."

"Promise?"

"Promise."

"Alright. I'm going to go get some tools to fix the front door, I'll be around if you need me okay?"

"Okay." The Baz closed his eyes and went back to sleep.

The thought occurred to Nial that The Baz would blame himself for Nial's sudden disappearance from Church End Estate. It would make sense that Nial would bail out of the squat and vanish without a trace after finding out his roommate was gay and in love with him. The situation provided convenient cover. The Baz would assume he screwed up by coming clean. He'd never come looking for Nial.

It should have made for a tidy bow on Nial's departure, but the thought of it pained him. He really did care for The Baz; he'd never intended to hurt him. He'd been careless. The Baz was collateral damage.

Downstairs, Nial examined the front door. The frame was badly splintered but he was confident there was still enough meat left on the jamb to fix the lock. Nial took a look around the house and realized he didn't have the tools at hand to fix it. Everything he had was on the job. The Baz didn't own so much as a screwdriver. He swept up the mess, pulled the door behind him, and took a stroll down the park to see if any of the other lads had a few tools lying around that he could borrow. He hadn't intended to learn a trade when he'd boarded the bus out of Ballygawley, but he'd leave this town with enough skill to call himself a carpenter… a carpenter with blood on his hands.

Chapter 15

"Look at the head on this hungry fucker," Shea said, a dishtowel draped over his shoulder as he opened the door to Nial. "You smelled the bolognese, I suppose? Hey, Tel," he called over his shoulder, "look at the head on this hungry cunt conveniently showing up at dinner time."

Terry popped a freshly washed head out of the bathroom down the hall to see who was at the door. "He looks like he could use a good meal that boyo."

"Come on in…" Shea said, grinning, "…til we get you fed."

Shea led the way back into the kitchen where he was attending to a huge pot of bolognese simmering on the stove.

"Any allergies I should know about?" He grinned, as he began crumbling about an eighth of black hash into the steaming pot.

"Nope, that looks good to me," Nial said, his nostrils

flaring at the smell of a hearty meal.

"Here…" Shea said, handing Nial the remainder of the nugget of hash. "Sit down there and roll us a wee joint and tell us all the craic."

Nial took the hash, sat at the kitchen table, and pulled a packet of rolling papers from his pocket. He never left home without a packet of rolling papers anymore. It had become part of his daily furniture: keys, cash, skins. You just never knew when you might need them.

He was astounded at how tidy the boys kept their little home. This was a squat. A place they didn't own, and yet it was spic and span, everything in its place: copper pots, pans, colanders… all sorts of knives and utensils. It was obvious Shea took his cooking very seriously.

"Here," Shea said, holding a wooden spoonful of bolognese over to Nial. "Take a wee taste of that."

Nial tasted the rich tomato sauce. It was delicious. He hadn't eaten a proper home-cooked meal since he'd left Tyrone. He'd been living out of the canteen at work, and in the evenings, fish and chips, or Chinese carryouts. Fixing the door to his own place could wait for an hour or two.

"You're some chef," Nial said as he went about the business of skinning a nice fat joint. "You should be doing this full time. Why the hell are you laying blocks?"

"Are you joking?" Shea said. "Do you know what they pay me to lay blocks in this town?"

Nial did know. Block layers were making almost twice as much as the best carpenters. Shea was making a small fortune.

Terry entered the kitchen pulling a fresh t-shirt over his wet head.

"How's life on the north end of the estate these days?"

"I came down looking for a few tools… a hammer… chisel… screwdriver…"

"You breaking into a new place already?"

"No, just fixing the one I have."

"What happened? You get broke into?"

"Sort of. Baz locked himself out, so he kicked in the door."

"Good man Baz." Shea laughed. Terry laughed too.

"That little fucker's crazy," said Terry.

"Knows how to get his hands on some decent hash though, I'll give him that," Shea said, nodding to the nugget of hash Nial held in his fingers. "Tel, get that man a glass of wine… you drink red?"

"I drank Thunderbird a few nights ago," Nail said. Thunderbird was the only wine he'd ever tasted.

"Not sure that counts as wine," said Shea. "I think Thunderbird might have a classification all its own. Let me see if I can find you a few hand tools."

Nial finished rolling he joint and held it up for inspection. "Will this do?"

"It'll have to do now I suppose," Terry said, pouring him a glass of wine. "Come on, take it into the front room and we'll sit for a minute before we eat."

Nial followed Terry on into the living room. The place was immaculate. Terry lifted a Fender off a wall rack and plugged it into a small amp next to the armchair. And as Nial lit the joint and took the first few drags, Terry played him a few bars of the most haunting music he'd ever heard.

"Man that's good," Nial said handing over the joint. "The hash?"

"No, the music… and the hash… you're really good, man. You should be in a band…"

"See!" Shea said, entering the room and handing Nial a few hand tools in a plastic shopping bag. "That's what I've been telling him, he's wasting his fucken talent. Got the long hair and the whole bit. Chicks go crazy for that shit. Good lookin' lad like you, long hair, guitar…"

"Fuck off," Tel said blushing.

"Look at this fucker," Shea said, shaking his head. "Hasn't a fucken clue what he has… I know if I looked like you and could play guitar like that I'd be in a rock band in a heartbeat."

Terry ignored them. He just went right on playing.

"See, fucken impossible with this one. Never listens. Wasted fucken talent. Here, give me that fucken joint," Shea said taking it directly from Terry's lips. "Don't fucken hog the whole thing."

"Thanks for the tools," Nial said, peering into the bag.

"Don't get caught by the cops walking up the park with that bag in your hand. They'll throw you in a cell for the night for intent."

"Intent for what?"

"Breaking and entering… I won't even carry my tool bag home to this estate… they catch you with that bag in your hand, you'll be in front of an English judge trying to explain yourself."

It might have been the weed, or the music… maybe it was the hash-laced bolognese… but the mention of cops and a judge sent Nial spiraling suddenly into a black hole of paranoia. He hadn't been thinking clearly. Or had he been? He couldn't decide. Of course on some level he'd understood that if he got caught buying a bomb he could go to jail, but had he really thought about it… really thought this whole thing through? This thing he was going to do could end his life. An English judge would lock him up and throw away the key if he was caught with a bomb in London. Even if he decided not to go get it tomorrow, maybe it could still be connected to him. What if Dessie was not really IRA at all? What if he was working undercover for the Brits? That would make sense. This whole situation was insanity… and The Baz… had he been neglectful in leaving him in a bed to sleep off a smack overload? Nial felt his heart began to pound in his chest. It was thundering like a spooked herd of buffalo. He could see it. His t-shirt was dancing on his chest. *Oh my God I'm having a fucking heart attack*, he thought, the panic rising in him, he was going to die, right here in this squat, with complete strangers, far from home… stoned.

"Hi boy, you alright there?" It was Shea; he was eyeing him curiously. "You alright?"

Nial stared at him but the words wouldn't come out.

"Hey Tel," Shea laughed. "Check out this one… he's stoned out of his tree. He's having a whitey. Can't even speak. Chill man… you're just stoned, you're alright. Just kick back there for a minute and relax… you're safe here… right Tel?"

"Yeah, man, just chill, you're all good here, you're among friends." Tel smiled.

"A whitey?" Nial managed to say.

"You're turning white..." said Terry. "You're panicking... but you're grand. You're just stoned."

"I'll get you a glass of water?" Shea said. "You lads about ready to eat. I'm fucken starvin' all of a sudden."

The mention of food began to draw Nial out of the black hole he'd dropped into. He could smell it now, the bolognese. The sweet aroma was bringing him back from the brink. Pretty soon it was all he could think about. His mouth was practically watering. The smell was overpowering... sweet tomatoes and garlic, all that delicious sauce... spaghetti... he wanted it now... in his mouth... NOW. He sprang from his chair and followed Shea to the kitchen.

"Looks like somebody's back to life," Tel said, putting his guitar back on the wall rack and following him into the kitchen.

Shea hit the button on the stereo on a shelf by the kitchen table and from the speakers drifted the first bars of "The Ghost in You" by Psychedelic Furs. The musical notes fluttered into the room in the form of tiny colorful birds, they circled the kitchen ceiling, dancing, spinning, swooping... a small blue bird, no bigger than a thimble, hovered in front of Nial's face and opened its tiny yellow beak and began to sing the first lines of the song. Nial began to laugh. He laughed, and he laughed, and he laughed. And when he tried to stop laughing, he laughed some more. It was the funniest thing he'd ever seen in his entire life. It was so funny, he needed it to stop but the bird kept on singing and Nial kept on laughing. Pretty soon Shea and Terry were laughing along with him. Nial managed to turn his head to see Terry, doubled over at the table, holding his sides, pleading, "Stop laughing… please… What are we laughing at?"

"I haven't a fucken clue, Tel," Shea managed to reply as tears streamed down his face as he braced himself at the kitchen counter.

"Please… stop… laughing," Terry was saying. "My sides hurt."

"I can't," Nial said…and they laughed like that the three of them for what seemed like an eternity. It was an exorcism of sorts, tears, snot, hands waving, an impossibility of joy and absurdity outside of the realm of all sense of normalcy… and it was good.

Shea was the first to regain composure. He stood upright and wiped the tears from his eyes and took a plate and started serving the food. "Holy fucken shit, I haven't laughed like that in a long time."

"What were we laughing at?" Terry said, still giggling.

"I haven't a fucking clue… he started it," Shea said, handing Nial a steaming plate of spaghetti bolognese. Nial's senses were overwhelmed with the aroma and a full-bodied sense of joy. If it were possible to stay right here in this kitchen, in this exact moment, he would never leave.

"Man, that is some good hash," he giggled, as his breathing returned to normal.

"That is some good shit." The other two agreed.

Nial reached for his fork to tackle the mountain of

food before him on the plate but Shea held up a finger....
"Ah, ah. Wait."

Shea finished serving Terry and himself, sat to the table, topped off the three wine glasses, raised his, and said, "I'd like to make a toast... To Church End Estate."

The other two clinked his glass and they drank.

"Now, tuck in lads."

After dinner and another three bottles of wine between them, Nial had discarded the idea of fixing the door. What did it matter! He'd be gone from London in a couple of days anyway. Best to enjoy a night like this when it presented itself. Shea suggested they head to The White Horse and that sounded like a perfect idea, so they went.

As they made their way down through the estate, Nial began to feel sad that this would be his last weekend here with this new family of people he'd met. This whacky crew felt like they could be his tribe. He felt free in their presence. This was a life beyond the gray confines of his past. Beyond the oppressive force of the North. Not one person had brought up religion, or politics, since he'd arrived in Church End Estate. Here in the estate they were free. Here in Church End Estate, they seemed to exist outside of societal norms. Sunday was just another day of the week, another day to be enjoyed, a day off work to relax and be with friends. No one ever mentioned going to mass. Growing up in the North, the entire week swung on Sunday like a pendulum. The week began and ended at Sunday morning mass. Everyone went to mass. Catholics to chapel. Protestants to church. It occurred to him for the first time that he'd never even bothered to ask Marissa her religion. Would it have mattered if she was Protestant? Of course it wouldn't. Not in the least.

Two cops strolled out of Taylors Lane just ahead of the boys. One of them was twirling a night stick as he clipped along. They stopped on the sidewalk in front of the three boys and the second cop pulled a small notebook and pen from his pocket.

"Evenin' gents. Where you lot off to tonight?"

None of the three responded.

"Alright then. Just want to ask you a few questions," said the one with the notebook. "We've had a few robberies around here of late. Houses being broken into when hard-working people are off at work. Valuables going missing. TVs, stereos, jewelry. You boys wouldn't know anything about that, would you?"

All three shook their heads.

"Course not. Course not." He sneered. "You three look like fine upstanding citizens…"

"We didn't do anything," Shea said. "This is harassment."

"Oh, you think you have rights here, do ya Paddy? I'll tell you what rights you have: whatever fucking rights I say you have. Now get your fucking hands up against the wall before I crack your skull open. All of ya."

Shea, Terry, and Nial turned without a word and placed their hands against the wall.

"You fucking Micks think you can come over 'ere

CHURCH END

and do whatever the fuck you like, do ya! Well, I got news for you, guv, this is my beat, and around here I make the rules."

The two cops patted them down roughly. Pulled cash from their pockets. Keys. Cigarettes. Lighters. Tossed everything they found on the sidewalk.

"Wot do we have here?" the taller of the two said pulling a pack of cigarette rolling papers from Shea's rear pocket.

"Is there a law against rolling your own tobacco in this country?" Shea said over his shoulder. The cop shoved him hard in the back.

"We better not find any drugs on you, boy, or you'll be one sorry little Mick I can tell you."

The two cops continued to search. Pulling their pockets inside out. Running fingers into the tops of their socks. Nial was beginning to worry that they would plant a little something just so that they could get Shea up to the station and into a cell alone for ten minutes.

Just then, a small entourage of about ten Belfast lads rounded the corner. Nial recognized them from The White Horse. Skinheads. Denim. Doc Martens. Hard men. The cops saw them too and they took a step back from the three boys. They waited to let the crew pass by, but the crew wasn't going anywhere.

"Move along," the taller of the two cops said weakly.

"Or what?" the big Belfast lad in front said. Nial knew the lad, Martin. He seemed to be their ringleader. A man not to be messed with.

"Who said that?" the cop said, even though it was

obvious that Martin had spoken. He wasn't hiding. There was a tense moment. The Belfast lads weren't going anywhere and the cops knew it.

"Alright there lads?" Martin called to the three against the wall.

"Just getting harassed here by these clowns," Shea said, turning from the wall.

"Get your hands back against the wall, Paddy," The cop snapped.

"What you just call him?" Martin said, taking a step forward, and the whole crew stepped forward with him.

There was a moment of complete silence. Martin was up on the cop. Face-to-face. Eye to eye. He wasn't going to go peacefully and everyone knew it. This could get ugly in a heartbeat. There were only two cops and about fifteen ablebodied Northern Irishmen, in a dimly lit alleyway. The wrong word right now would be like striking a match in a dynamite factory.

"Go on. Get out of here," the tall cop said, puffing his chest out best he could, trying to save some shred of his dignity in the face of obvious defeat. Then directly to Martin, "You better watch your back, boy."

"I'm not your fucken boy," Martin said, taking another quick step forward until he was practically touching the cop's nose. The two men stood there face-to-face. The energy of a thousand years of oppressor and oppressed sparking between them like some cosmic lightning storm.

"Okay, everybody, on your way now, that's it," the smaller of the two cops said. "Let's go. Everybody, just on our way. Come on. Off you go." Terry, Shea, and Nial gathered their belongings off the sidewalk and the two parties separated. Cops going one way, the Northerners on toward The White Horse.

"I got your number, Paddy," the cop called after them when they were at a safe distance. Martin turned, sneering, and held his middle finger aloft.

"Anytime you think you're fit, wanker," Martin said.

"Thanks lads," Shea said, as he spat about a quarter of black hash out of the corner of his mouth into the palm of his hand. "Thought for sure I was going to have to swallow it there for a minute. First round's on me."

The lads laughed. Martin, locked his arm around Shea's head and pulled him into a headlock. "You mad Tyrone bastard."

They moved on through the estate like that. A wild, untamable tribe. And Nial felt proud to be among them. These truly were his people.

Chapter 16

It was almost eleven o'clock before Nial spotted Marissa entering The White Horse alone. Nial was standing at the bar with Shea and Terry still nursing their first pint. The hash they had eaten in the bolognese had hit all of them with a wallop as soon as they'd arrived in the bar. They were rendered speechless. Seeing Marissa, Nial felt the first sense that the initial wave had subsided, and he lifted the pint to his lips realizing his mouth had gone bone dry in the interim. Marissa was glowing. She was wearing a white t-shirt that hugged her body tightly. Her dark, wavy hair was practically shining as she lifted it back over her shoulder. She glanced around the bar and met his eyes for just a second, but she turned away again without giving him even the slightest instant to transmit how much he missed her.

Nial turned to Shea and Terry and he hoped he didn't look as stoned as they did. Terry's eyes were practically closed. Shea's head drooped a little as he nodded to the sound of whatever was playing on the jukebox. The sorry sight of the two of them made him snap out of his stoned state. He hoped Marissa hadn't seen in him just now what he could see in them. They were a pretty pathetic sight. He felt a wave of nausea and made a beeline for the door. He needed fresh air in his lungs, now.

Outside, he braced himself against a wall and took a few deep breaths. The door opened behind him and Marissa appeared.

"Jesus, Pat. Are you okay?" she said.

He shook his head.

"What are you on?"

"I had dinner with the lads… There might have been a little hash in the bolognese."

"A little?"

"Maybe it was a lot."

"Are you going to be okay?"

"I'm grand. It was just… it was seeing you…" He stopped and shook his head.

"Are you going back in?"

"No. I think maybe I should go home."

"You sure you're okay?"

"Yes. I'm fine. I'm alright now. How are you?"

"In better shape than you are, that's for sure."

Nial managed a laugh. She smiled too.

"It's good to see you," he said.

"Yeah, it's good to see you too."

"You want to walk with me for a wee bit?"

"A wee bit? You asking me to go home with you?"

"Maybe," Nial smiled. "That would be nice."

"Come on," she said, taking his hand in hers. "I'll

walk with you for a wee bit."

They were only walking for a few steps before Marissa lifted his arm and draped it around her shoulder and tucked in next to him. A few steps more and they were pressed into the doorway of a shop smothering each other in kisses. Half an hour later they were wrapped around each other on her bed, sharing a cigarette.

"I missed you," Nial said.

"You're a strange one, alright. I can't quite seem to get at the heart of you at all. Why won't you let me in?"

"I'm trying. I'm really trying. I want to."

"So what's the problem?"

"There's stuff I can't tell you."

"What are you so afraid will happen?"

"Maybe you'd hate me. Maybe. I can't talk about it."

"Jesus Pat…"

"Give me one week. One week and I'll tell you everything."

"One week for what? Tell me."

"I can't."

"What the hell is this big mystery?"

"One week. Give me one week and I promise I'll tell you."

"Okay, you have one week. That's it. Wait, you're not going to do something stupid or dangerous over the next few days are you?"

"One week."

"Don't go doing something stupid."

"Let's just talk about it in a week. I can't say anything more right now. Stop, I shouldn't have said anything at all."

CHURCH END

"Okay," Missy said, seeing the fear in him, feeling his body tense next to hers. "I won't ask again, I promise. One week."

"One week," he said, and he wrapped his arms around her and held her to him as if she were a shield.

Chapter 17

"Fuck. What time is it?" Marissa said sitting bolt upright in the bed. A rare and marvelous bar of sunlight had found her still wrapped in Nial's arms. She leapt from the bed and began digging in a drawer for clean clothes. "Shit, I really have to run. Don't you have to be at work?"

"Maybe I'll take the day off. Come back to bed."

"Out. Now."

"I should probably go back home and make sure Baz is still breathing," Nial said, rising from the bed, the glare of the sun suddenly piercing his skull as he came crashing back to the realization that today was the day he would hold a bomb in his hands. "Jesus, some friend I am."

"You're the only friend he has left."

Nial dressed hurriedly. He felt cold, raw, hungover, and guilty. He was already living with the sin of the act he planned on committing. Without a drink to soften the jagged edge, the lie ate into him.

Marissa seemed to sense he was pulling away, and she slipped up behind him and wrapped her arms around his waist.

"I don't know what your game is, and I'm not going to ask you to tell me, but I want you to know I care what happens to you now… be careful. Please"

"Okay." he managed to say, and he turned to her. They held each other for a moment before Nial turned and slipped out of the house without another word.

Baz was still exactly where Nial had left him in the bed. He stirred and opened his eyes as Nial tried to close the bedroom door behind him to slip away.

"Hey."

"Hey."

"How you feel this morning? You okay?"

"I feel like I'm going to die."

"Let me get you a glass of water." Nial went away and came back with a pint glass of cold water. The Baz propped himself up in the bed and started glugging it thirstily.

"Do yourself a favor and lay low today. Stay in bed. Drink water. Sweat it out a bit."

"I don't feel good."

"You will. You'll be okay. You just have to hold out for a bit. Do you have any money to get yourself something to eat?"

Baz avoided his eyes and shook his head. Nial

pulled twenty pounds from his pocket and set it on the bed next to him. "That's for food. Okay! Food, only."

The Baz nodded weakly.

"I have to go to work. When I come back, I'll take you out for a decent dinner... on me."

"Thank you, Pat."

"No problem."

Nial was about to leave the room when Baz said, "Hey, remember when I told you that story... about that Ecuadorian girl..."

"...Emmanuel?" Nial said.

"It wasn't a girl."

Nial smiled. "That makes sense. I'll catch you later?"

Nial locked himself in the bathroom for a minute, retrieved the envelope of cash, and tucked the fat wad into his front pocket.

Out on Church Road he was just in time to catch the twenty-two bus to Wilsden Green. He could take the train from there.

This would be his last day on the job in London. If everything went according to plan, he would have the bomb in the mail to Anderson that evening. Monday he would be in Shepherd's Bush to watch the mailman deliver the package to Anderson's repair shop. Then he would have to find Marissa and tell her the truth... or leave London without saying goodbye to anyone.

At lunchtime on the site, Nial invited The Burner out for

a pint. He felt indebted to the old man and wanted to thank him in some small way for taking him under his wing, teaching him the basics of the trade, sharing some small inkling of his wisdom. He'd grown very fond of The Burner. Burner had treated him with respect from the outset. Treated him like an equal. He would miss him.

Once they were seated with their pints in an empty corner booth at The Red Lion, Nial raised his glass.

"Thank you," he said. The Burner eyed him with some curiosity.

"What's this all about?"

"I just wanted to say thank you."

"For what?"

"For teaching me how to be a carpenter."

"You're a carpenter?"

Nial laughed. "Well, for giving me an introduction to the trade."

"You're welcome." Burner smiled and he tapped Nial's pint glass with his own.

The old Irishman they'd watched from the window digging in the rain appeared at their table with two fresh pints. "Yis'll have a wee sup on me," he said, giving them a wink.

"No call for that now…" Burner started, but the man was moving away again, giggling to himself as if he'd been running the image of the cement bag landing on the foreman's head in repeat ever since.

"You made a believer out of that man," said The Burner in that rhetorical way he had of talking sometimes like he was just thinking a thing through for himself. "Put a sense of justice back in his world. Like God dropped that bag of cement out of heaven just for him."

"It didn't look terribly spiritual from where I was standing," Nial said, but The Burner wasn't listening, he was still working through his through process, teasing it out til the end.

"But he'll wake up in his bedsit alone one of these mornings though, hungover, broke, seventy years old, his body not fit for the spade, nobody back home that would have him anymore, and he'll realize the Godly thing would have been to try and help that man." The Burner lifted the fresh pint the man had brought for him and paused as if considering the point of his little sermon. "Revenge is sweet… but by God it's costly."

He turned to Nial then as if he'd just remembered that he was sitting there. Held his pint toward him in the manner of a toast and said, "If there's to be panic, let it be organized."

Nial hadn't the slightest clue what that meant, but he liked the sound of it. He tapped his pint off The Burner's and tipped the rest of the pint to his head. He was going to miss spending time with this wise old sage.

By the time Nial decided to make his way back across the street to the site to pick up his tool bag, he had quite the buzz onboard. The Burner did not come with him. He'd made a last-minute decision to stay where he was. "I'm not a drinking man," he'd said as Nial got up to leave the table. "But when I have a drink, I have a drink.

I'll see you bright and early Monday morning."

"See you Monday," Nial said. Sad to have to lie to his old friend. He would likely never see him again.

Chapter 18

An hour later Nial was leaning against a wall outside Chi Chi's Mexican restaurant in Leicester Square, his tool bag resting between his feet. It had just turned five o'clock and the streets were crammed with pedestrians rushing home for the weekend. Businessmen in dark suits hurried by with briefcases under their arms. A woman wielding a severe-looking wooden-handled umbrella. A handful of Irish construction workers, boots and jeans covered in cement dust. One of the lads gave Nial a nod, recognizing him as one of the tribe. Nial nodded back. It had never occurred to him that Irish people had a look. That they would stand out. It made him self-conscious, especially when he was on the Tube, covered in sawdust from the job. In the eyes of the English straphangers, he was a Paddy. It gave him no comfort to know that he stood apart from the crowd right now.

Luckily the evening was beginning to turn dark already. He welcomed the dusk. Streetlights flickered on around the square. Chatty couples were stopping into lighted bars. A small crowd was already beginning to form outside the American Steakhouse at the top of the square, even Chi Chi's was almost at max capacity already. A line had formed at the ticket booth of the cinema next door for the early show. They were showing *Hannah and Her Sisters*. Nial was tempted to lift his tool bag and join the queue. He loved Woody Allen movies. He could disappear into the dark theatre with a bucket of popcorn, a large Coke. He had thirteen hundred pounds in cash in his pocket. He could do anything he wanted. He could get on the train right now and head straight for Heathrow with his tool bag. He'd be out of London ahead of the game. Enough in his pocket to buy a nice used car, a bag of tools to get started as a carpenter. This could be a fresh start. He could surprise his parents. He could just imagine the delight on his mother's face.

"Are you Pat?"

A man had stopped in front of him. He was wearing a dark hood, his head slightly bowed. His face was a shadow.

"I am," Nial managed to say.

The man hunkered down and slipped a small package into the tool bag between Nial's feet, and he zippered it closed and stood up again, keeping his head bowed.

"You have something for me?"

Nial handed him the envelope that held a thousand pounds of his hard-earned cash. The man shoved it into a side pocket of his coat.

"The minute the box is opened: bang." The man turned and he was gone.

***

All around him the Friday evening crowd continued to buzz on: voices, laughter, traffic, music... but the entire scene had taken on a sinister, cartoonish appearance. Nial took a look down at the bag between his feet. There was a bomb sitting between his legs. One wrong move and there would be carnage on the square. He looked up and a passing policeman gave him a curious glance. He froze, trying to look as casual as possible. The policeman walked on. Nial leaned down and took the strap of his tool bag and raised it carefully, placing it over his shoulder. The tools fell together in the bag, a hammer clinked off a chisel and a shock ran down his arm. He placed an arm around the bag and held it snug against his chest, cradling it like you would a newborn.

He took the train two nerve-racking stops to Green Park and with all the tenderness he could muster, he inched his way to the Jubilee line for the transfer, hugging the wall as he went for fear some passing commuter might slam into the bag while rushing past. He imagined the headlines: "IRA Bomb Kills Hundreds in Friday Evening Massacre." This was how these things happened, he thought, this was how innocent people wound up dead, exactly like this: idiots with explosives, making poor decisions.

As he stood in the crowded carriage on the Jubilee line it occurred to him that the bomb might well be set to explode in his arms. Perhaps he had unwittingly become a pawn in a much larger struggle. Maybe it was supposed to go off on a crowded train. Maybe they just needed some dumb sucker to carry it. A woman in the seat next to him was nursing a small child. She glanced at Nial just then and catching his eye, gave him a motherly smile.

He needed to get off this train.

When they pulled into Baker Street, the doors opened and a mad rush of commuters started shoving past him to get onboard. Nial clutched the bag tightly to his chest and forged his way through them and onto the platform. The train doors closed behind him and he stood there for a moment to catch his breath and his composure. In front of him a tile mural of Sherlock Holmes looked on, a plume of smoke rising from his bulbous pipe, as if to say: *Well, well, what do we have here?*

When he exited the station, Nial made a beeline for the first black cab he saw parked outside. He settled into the big back seat keeping the toolbelt still held firmly in his lap.

"Where to guv?"

"Harlesden please, and could you take it easy? I'm not feeling too good."

"Youse not going to throw up in my car, is ya?"

"No. No, I'm fine. I'd just appreciate it if you could drive slowly, that's all."

The driver half turned to give Nial a once-over. He glanced down at the tool bag, at his dusty boots and worried expression, figured him for one more drunk Mick, turned, hit the meter, and eased into Friday evening traffic.

"You got a bomb in that bag, Paddy?"

Nial thought he'd misheard him.

"I'm sorry?"

"I said, looks like you got a bomb in that bag, the way you're hanging on to it."

"Aye, it's a bomb. One wrong move and we're both fucked," Nial said, forcing a smile.

The driver regarded him in the rearview mirror, muttered something about Paddies, then reached for the radio to turn up Bronski Beat, "Smalltown Boy," to drown out any further conversation.

Chapter 19

When they reached Church Road, Nial had the driver drop him outside of the estate. He paid and stood on the street checking his change until the cab was out of sight. Then he made his way back to the squat.

The door opened with a light shove. Still no lock. The place was quiet as a grave.

"Hello. Baz. Anyone home?" Nial called, sounding his way as he closed the door behind him. There wasn't so much as a creak in the place.

He took the tool bag to his room and set it down carefully on the mattress. Gingerly, he inched open the zipper and with bated breath he lifted the small package. It was a padded envelope, about eight inches by six, that looked like it held a small, firm brick of some sort. To his surprise he saw that it had been left unsealed. Nial turned the envelope in his hands and inside he could see the end of what looked like a polished block of cherrywood. He sat it on the bed and stepped away from it. He was uncertain of how to proceed from here. Was the envelope supposed to be open? Was he supposed to take this thing out of the envelope? Were there further instructions tucked into the envelope next to the box or underneath it? He had been given no direction on how to deal with this thing. What had the man said: "The minute the box is opened: bang." The box. It's a box. He said the box needed to be opened. Of course. He went back to the envelope and, kneeling beside it, slowly slid it out onto the floor.

Sure enough, it was a small cherrywood jewelry box with a bright, shiny brass clasp on its front and a rose hand-carved into the lid. It was perfectly crafted. Not a blemish. His few weeks as a carpenter had given him a new appreciation for the thing. It was an admirable piece of woodworking. The brass clip compelled him to reach for it. To flip it open, to see what treasure it beheld within. The rose on top spoke of love. This was a gift. It was genius. The brass clasp was a question that demanded an answer. There was no way Anderson would be able to resist flipping it open. Then: bang.

Nial ran his fingers across the engraved rose. "This is for you, Cathal," he whispered. He'd need some tape to close the envelope. A marker to address it to Anderson. And stamps. How many? He'd stick an entire book of stamps on it just in case. He glanced at his watch. It was still only six o'clock. There was a small stationery store right across Church Road. If he hurried he still might get it into a mailbox for late pickup.

He slipped the envelope under the corner of the bedsheet and dashed out of the squat and went bounding down the stairwell taking four steps at a time.

He was standing at the counter paying for the tape and stamps when someone slipped their hands over his eyes from behind. He was startled but he remained clam. Obviously it was someone who knew him. The hands were soft. A woman's. The person inched closer to him and pressed against his back. He could feel the softness of her breasts against his upper back. There was only one woman in all of England who would stand this close to him in a store.

"I'd recognize those hands anywhere. Mum, is that you?"

"You are a very disturbed young man, Pat Coyle," Marissa said, as he turned to her. She took his face in her hands and kissed him. The shopkeeper, a cardiganed English lady, peered over the top of a pair of thick black spectacles.

"That'll be two pounds fifty-three," she said, putting the stamps and black marker into a wrinkled brown paper bag.

"Somebody's birthday back home?" Marissa said, fishing for another thread into Nial's story.

"Something like that," Nial said, handing the lady three pounds.

"What do you mean something like that? It's either somebody's birthday or it's not."

"It's not."

"Okay."

"I just have a couple of wee things to mail, that's all."

"What wee things?" Marissa asked.

"Jesus… just some things," Nial snapped. Marissa turned sharply and walked out of the store. The lady handed Nial his change with a scowl. He took it, and the bag, and hurried out after Marissa. She was waiting for him.

"What are you hiding? This is all part of the big secret, right?" She was upset. He'd been an ass.

"I'm sorry. I'll tell you everything on Monday evening. Tuesday at the latest. Just give me a few days."

She searched his face for some further clue but there were no answers there.

"I have to go," she said. "I have to run home and get changed. I told Decco I'd meet him for a drink in The Horse. You coming?"

"I have a few things to do at the house. I'll get cleaned up…"

"Suit yourself," she said, turning away.

"Marissa…" he called after her, but he didn't have the rest of the sentence at hand. She turned and gave him a sad smile and kept on her way. "I'll be there in an hour."

Nial hurried across the dual carriageway. He was determined to get this thing out of his hands and into the mail. Maybe then he'd feel rid of it. Maybe then he could let Marissa know how he really felt about her.

When he got back, the squat was as quiet as he left it. He could picture Anderson in his store holding the package in his hands, maybe a cup of tea next to him on a workbench, the radio playing, the simplicity of the knife being slid into the sealed crease to open it. Nial noticed the kitchen light on. He paused for a moment in the hallway. He couldn't remember if it was on when he left. It gave him an uneasy feeling. He stood there for a moment. Silence.

He went on to the front room and hunkered by the bed and pulled back the blanket. The package was gone. He pulled the blanket off the mattress. It was impossible. It had to be here. He glanced around the room. Maybe he hadn't put in the bed. There was a noise in the front hallway and he jumped up and ran to the hallway. The front door was thrown wide open. He heard footsteps running across the landing. He ran to the door just in time to see The Baz disappear into the stairwell with the package tucked under his arm.

"Baz…" he yelled. But he heard the footsteps hammering down the stairs. Baz was not stopping for anything. Nial glanced over the balcony railing as he began his pursuit. A young couple had just stepped out of a car downstairs. The father opened the back door of the car and two young children, a boy and a girl, spilled out, laughing, one chasing the other toward the stairwell. Baz almost tumbled into them dashing past, then he was out of sight.

"Baz, don't." Nial bounded for the stairwell. He had to catch him. He took the stairs five at a time, his brain trying to catch up to the impossibility of the situation. In a flash he was downstairs, just in time to catch sight of Baz disappearing into an alleyway about fifty feet away. He sprinted after him with everything he had in him. When he came out the other end of the short walkway, Baz was gone. He glanced around at a wide open square between four rows of houses, trying to decide which direction to take next. There were three other alleyways off this square. The Baz could have taken any of them. There was no time to stop and think about where they might lead; he had to keep running.

When he reached the end of the next alleyway, he froze. The same two cops who had stopped him, only nights before, had Baz up against a wall about a hundred yards away. The taller of the two was patting him down. The other already had the package in his hands and was peering into it. Nial instinctively took a few steps back until he was concealed from view in the alleyway. He was breathing heavily. His heart was thundering in his chest. He had to do something, fast. The jig was up. He had to stop them from opening the box. He peeked around the corner of the building and the cop had dropped to a hunker and was inching the box out of the envelope. The Baz glanced over his shoulder, looked down at the cop, and then he looked up and right at Nial, and seeing him, he grinned, just as the cop popped open the clasp on the small cherrywood box.

The blast shook the wall Nial was leaning against. Nial turned away to shield his face from the carnage. He didn't have the strength to look back again, instead he just started walking, back the way he had come. The world had been reduced to a high-pitched singing in his ears. People were running toward the source of the explosion. A muffled alarm sounded somewhere behind him. Nial kept walking toward Marissa's place. He needed to find her right away.

When he turned the corner near her flat, he saw her. Like everyone else she was running toward the sound of the explosion. She ran to him, wrapped her arms around him and started smothering his face in kisses. She was speaking to him, but Nial couldn't hear anything she was saying. She could see that he had witnessed whatever had happened. It was in his face. She hooked her arm into his and led him back into her home.

She sat him on the bed and got a glass of water for him.

He took a sip and his hearing started to come back. Outside he heard sirens. Distant screams.

"Can you hear me?" she was saying. "Are you okay?"

"I'm in trouble."

"What happened? What did you do?"

"I had a bomb. The Baz is dead. There were two cops…"

"What!" She peered into his eyes. "What did you say?"

"I think I killed them."

Marissa slowly dropped to her knees and buried her face in her hands.

"It's my fault."

Marissa dropped her hands to her thighs and stared at him for a moment, then she rose and put her hands on his shoulders and looked him square in the eyes and said, "We need to get out of here. Now."

Without another word, she grabbed a large duffle bag out of a closet and began shoving clothes into it. She hunkered next to the bed and shoved her arm under the mattress and produced a fat envelope of cash.

"I think I killed them," Nial repeated to no one in particular.

Marissa flung the duffle bag over her shoulder and

grabbed Nial by the arm. "Get up."

"Where are we going?"

"Just move."

Nial got up and made his way down the stairs ahead of her. Marissa ran back and came out of the room with a box of detergent.

"Are you doing laundry?"

"Just stay next to me and keep walking," she said, opening the door of the flat and outside into the chaos. The air was thick with the blare of sirens, police cars, fire trucks. A helicopter was already hovering overhead. People were running from all directions into the park, trying to get close to the source of the explosion. The police were already trying to set up a barrier to stop the flow of traffic into the crime scene.

A cop with a bullhorn started yelling.

"Everyone, stay back. Back behind the barriers."

They were hurrying to create a perimeter. Two cops had already begun interviewing anyone exiting Church End Estate.

"You live here?" a cop asked Nial when they reached him.

"We live right there," Marissa said, pointing in a general way to the flats.

"Did you see what happened?"

"No. What did happen? We just came out to do laundry. Was there an accident?"

"You didn't hear anything?" the cop asked. He was young. He looked harried. Unsure of himself.

"I heard sirens," Nial said.

A reporter from the BBC ran up with a cameraman in tow.

CHURCH END

"What can you tell us about what's happened here today?" she said, shoving the microphone in the young cop's face.

"I don't know. Maybe take a step…"

"Is it true that there was an explosion? Can you confirm any fatalities?"

The young cop was glancing around for assistance. It was obvious he was in way over his head. Marissa took Nial's hand in hers and started leading him away from the chaos. The cop was too busy dealing with the camera in his face to notice they were gone.

Church Road was in pandemonium. Emergency vehicles and spectators were rushing to the scene from every direction. Nial held onto Marissa's hand and followed her on down the street, through the gathering crowd. Past The White Horse and the laundromat and on toward Wilsden. He had no idea where they were going. He only knew that they had to get away.

Chapter 20

They were almost in Wilsden, still walking, when Nial heard his name being called from behind. Not Pat. His real name: Nial.

"Nial. Hey, Nial!" Marissa stopped to stare at the boy who was running to catch up with them. Nial tried to ignore him. Tried to keep on walking, but the boy could not be deterred. "Nial," the boy said, bounding up alongside them to make himself known. "It's me, Killian. We went to school together at Saint Ciaran's."

There was no avoiding it. The boy was standing beside them. He looked happy to see a familiar face from back home.

"Oh, hey, Killian. How are you, man?" Nial said, feigning enthusiasm. He and the boy were not close friends but they'd been in the same grade together for five years through high school. He needed to acknowledge him and get out of the situation as quickly as possible so he could start explaining to Marissa what was going on.

He'd kept her in the dark too long already. It was time to come clean. She stood silent, a closed-lip smile on her face.

"This is Marissa," Nial said, seeing that Killian was glancing to her for an introduction.

"Oh, hi luv, nice to meet ya." Nial was taken aback by Killian's Cockney accent but he cast it aside. There was too much else going on to fully acknowledge it.

Marissa nodded her head at Killian, but said nothing.

"So, wot, you're livin' ova 'ere now is ya? Cor blimey, can't believe it's you?" said Killian, excitedly. "You live 'round 'ere then, does ya?"

"Excuse me," Marissa said. "I thought you said you two went to school together."

"Yeah, we did 'n all luv…" Killian said playfully punching Nial on the shoulder.

"So what's with the fucking Brit accent?" Marissa said, harshly.

"You wha'?" Killian said, taken aback.

"You heard me. What's with the fucken Brit accent? You ashamed of your own accent? Your own not good enough for you?"

"Oy, blimey, hold up there, sweetheart."

"Don't you fucken sweetheart me, you little fuck. Take your phony Cockney accent and fuck the fuck off."

"'Ere, ah… hang about…" Killian stammered, but Marissa was not having any of it. She took a step toward him.

"Fuck off, you Limey cunt," she spat.

Killian looked to Nial for some show of support, but got none.

"She's right," Nial added. "You are a bit of a cunt. Maybe you better fuck off."

Killian seemed stunned. Nial braced himself for a punch, but Killian just shook his head in disbelief, then stepped around them and walked off. They turned to watch him go. When he was a good hundred feet away, he turned and yelled back, "Assholes." Then he spun around and ran away.

Marissa turned back to face Nial.

"So, Nial, you want to tell me what the fuck is going on?"

"I told you I'd tell you everything. And I will. I promise."

"I'm listening."

"Can we sit down somewhere?"

"Now?"

"Come on. Let's get off the street. There's a pub right there," Nial said pointing to a restaurant bar called The Kings Arms on the next corner. "Let's go in and sit down, have a drink and I'll tell you everything."

"No more lies."

"No more lies."

They found a quiet booth in the back of The Kings Arms and Nial brought the drinks to the table. He sat across from Marissa, took a sip from his pint, and he began telling her the whole story: his brother Cathal, Anderson, Dessie, the bomb… all of it. Marissa never once interrupted him. She sipped her gin and bitters and she listened intently. When she could see that he was done, she reached across the table and took his hand in hers and held it.

"I'm sorry about your brother."

"And now, Baz is dead."

"It wasn't your fault."

"It's my fault."

"He stole from you. You didn't kill him."

"And those cops… what did they do?"

"We need to get out of London."

"You'd come with me?"

"If you wanted me to."

"Yes," Nial said, and he reached over and kissed her. "Where would we go?

"America."

"America?"

"Why not! I've been saving for it. We could go to New York, or San Francisco… far away from here."

"Where would we stay? Do you know anyone over there?"

"I have… fuck…"

"What?"

"My address book, my passport. I left them in my room," Marissa said burying her face in her hands.

"You can't go back."

"I have to go back. I need my papers. I can't get to America without my passport. I'll wait til morning. They're not looking for me. They're looking for you. I need my passport."

"I don't have a passport, or enough money to get us both to New York."

"I have enough to get us there. Tomorrow we go to the embassy… We'll get you a passport."

"What if they're looking for me?"

"They don't even have your real name. No one knows who you are."

A round-faced waitress with dark eye makeup and a wild, untamed mass of hair who looked like she might be a roadie for The Cure stopped at their table. "Ready for another one?"

"No. We're actually looking for a place to stay for the night. Something low-key. Local. A hotel. Bed and breakfast," Marissa said.

The girl had the sullen countenance of a depressed thirteen-year-old.

"Down the street. Next corner. Bed and breakfast." She groaned, before turning away with a contemptuous eyeroll.

Outside, dark had descended. They walked to the corner of the block in silence. The bed and breakfast was in a nondescript brown brick townhouse owned by a sweet old man. He asked no questions. Gave them no sense that he cared if they were who they said they were. He walked them to the top of the stairs and opened the door to a large, clean, comfortable room in the back of the house. He handed Marissa the key and left them alone.

Once they were alone in the room Nial fell onto the bed. He was exhausted. He closed his eyes and held the pillow to his face. Marissa laid on the bed next to him but she didn't touch him. Before he lifted his head he could hear the shift in her breathing. She was asleep.

He lay next to her in silence watching the moon out the open window. Baz was dead, and it was entirely his fault. Baz was dead because Nial had intended to take another man's life. Was this how God served justice, he wondered? Is this how you damned your soul from joy… by crossing the spiritual divide into the realm of murder? No, he hadn't actually murdered Anderson yet, but he'd wanted to. The intention was there. He would have killed him if it had worked out. Isn't that the same thing in God's eyes? Was that enough? The thought? He sat with a start and physically shook his head as if he could dislodge the thought process from its dark path. Marissa felt him move. She sat up behind him and wrapped her arms around his waist.

"Shhhhhh. It's okay. It's okay." she said, rocking him softly. He turned to her with tears in his eyes and held her face in his hands, looked down into her soul. She was still pure. She was still clean of this darkness, he kissed her mouth and felt her tongue on his, he wanted to disappear inside her, hide every part of himself in the universe of her warmth… and for a short while it worked, for a short while he was no longer a banished soul… for a short while, he was free again.

Chapter 21

The following morning after breakfast, Marissa left to return to the squat for her passport, alone. Nial walked her to the bus stop and hugged her goodbye, made her promise to come back to him, then he bought the morning newspapers at the corner shop and returned to his room at the B&B.

The explosion in Church End Estate had made front page in all the dailies. One headline read "IRA Bomb Massacre." Another pronounced: "Massacre On The Mainland." Nial pored through every line searching for details. Baz was dead, but it looked as though both policemen had survived the blast. One article described their condition as "severe but stable." Another piece suggested that one may never walk again, another that both men had lost their sight. Of course it would be too early to know how bad their injuries really were, but Nial felt some slim sense of relief that both policemen were still alive. Was one death less weight on his soul?

CHURCH END

He imagined it had to be. If he imagined it had to be then maybe that made it so.

Each of the articles he read stated that the IRA had not yet claimed responsibility for the bombing. Well of course they hadn't: they didn't do it. But the bomb fragments found at the scene indicated that this was a device commonly used by the Provos.

Another prominent newspaper stated that it appeared the explosion was intended for somewhere else. Then went to on to speculate on the possibility that it was intended to assassinate Prime Minister Margaret Thatcher in her home at 10 Downing Street in retaliation for her brutal policing tactics in Northern Ireland. The narrative also suggested that the dead bomber was a mastermind responsible for at least three other IRA bombings on the mainland. A collage of grainy photos accompanied the piece: the rubble of a bar destroyed in an explosion… paramedics carrying a bloodied corpse on a stretcher, and a black-and-white photograph of the cherubic assassin: Barry Callaghan. Scotland Yard had released a statement saying that they had reason to believe the bomber's accomplices were still in London and that they would not escape justice.

Nial fell onto his back on the bed. His head was spinning. He felt nauseous. They had pinned so much to The Baz. They would go after his family now too. They'd be looking for any thread that would lead them to the roommate who'd suddenly disappeared. What did they have on him if they searched the squat? Nothing. Fingerprints maybe. But he wasn't a part of any fingerprint database. They'd track him back to McGinley's.

But he'd given a false name there, and Dessie would surely cover for him to save his own ass. Nial sat up again. He hadn't eaten breakfast. He wasn't hungry, but he had the sudden thought that maybe the little old man who'd shown them to their room might be downstairs right now also reading the same newspapers and thinking about the two strangers upstairs who'd paid for bed and breakfast but were not yet down for breakfast. He got up and made for the door. He had to stay smart. He had to stay ahead of this thing if they were to make it out of London.

Downstairs in the small front dining area, Nial took a seat by the front window facing the street. He could see the bus stop from there.

"Ah, there you are…" the old man said softly as he appeared from behind a closed door. "Tea?"

"That would be lovely."

"For two?"

"Just the one for now, thanks."

"One tea coming up." And away he went again.

A few minutes later he was back with a tray. He stood by the table balancing it in one hand and began placing the fine china setting in front of Nial just so. There were fluffy scrambled eggs, bacon, sausage, and a slice of fried tomato. Two slices of buttered toast. And a tall, slim glass of freshly squeezed orange juice. Nial had not intended to eat but the rich smell of food and the pleasant presentation reminded him that a decent meal had not crossed his lips in some time.

"Thank you. This looks amazing."

"You're welcome." The old man smiled. He was

wearing a sharp white shirt under a blue wool vest. And when he reached to pour Nial's tea, Nial caught the faint scent of marzipan off his sleeve. "Should I keep the pot on the boil for your friend?"

"No thanks. She had to pop out to see a friend. She'll be back a little later."

"Will you be with me another night then?"

"I believe we will. It'll be hard to leave with this kind of service."

The old man laughed softly. "Well, you need anything else, just come on down and let me know. I'll be in the kitchen, or out back in the garden tending my roses."

"Thank you," Nial said, feeling a sense of relief that at least here he could feel safe for now.

The breakfast was superb. He thought of all the money he'd wasted drinking since he'd been in London. He could have been seeing the country. Train trips somewhere new every weekend. Treating himself to little bed and breakfasts like this everywhere he went. There were a thousand ways to rob yourself of delightful existence, he decided.

By twelve thirty Marissa had not returned. She'd been gone since before nine that morning. That was more than three hours ago. She should have been back. Maybe the police had pulled her in for questioning. Or worse, maybe Dessie had been waiting for her at her flat. Nial had never mentioned her name to Dessie of course but that wouldn't mean he hadn't figured that part out for himself. He had a bad feeling that something was not right. It shouldn't have taken her more than an hour to go there and come back. Something must have happened. He would have to go find her.

At one o'clock he left a note on the bed for her explaining that he'd gone up to Harlesden to look for her, and if she returned to the room to just wait there for his return. He went downstairs and found Roger in the back garden pruning a rose bush just as he said. Nial explained he'd be out for a little while but would definitely be staying on for another night. He offered to pay in advance but Roger waved him away with his pruning shears saying that tomorrow would be time enough for that. Once more Nial felt the sting of his kindness... another fine Englishman who didn't deserve his rage.

On the bus ride to Harlesden Nial tried sat downstairs in the back near the exit. He had no idea what to expect when he got to the estate. Everything was out of whack. He had nothing solid to ground himself to anymore. He leaned his face against the window and looked out at the huddle of gray clouds stampeding over London. He thought of Baz. He thought of how he first appeared when he'd met him on the ferry... this otherworldly creature... his willingness to trust... his generosity... his smile. Nial had robbed the world of someone special... a true original... for the first time since the explosion, Nial began to sob. Baz was his friend. And now he was dead.

A little old lady in a headscarf leaned over and handed Nial a tissue paper she'd taken from her purse. He took it and tried to respond but the words came out in an embarrassing snot-filled blubber... she raised her hand as if to say, *It's okay, you don't have to explain it*. The bus lurched to a stop at a light and Nial bolted for the door. The conductor yelled for him to stop but he was gone running down a side street where he collapsed in a doorway and wept.

When he gathered himself a few minutes later he realized he was only a few blocks from the White Horse. He dusted himself off. Took a deep breath and made himself a vow to try and keep it all together long enough to find Marissa and get her safely out of London.

As he crossed Church Road a cop car tore past with the siren screaming. The car had come out of the estate. Maybe it was related to what had happened here yesterday, or maybe it wasn't. The news crews were gone. By all exterior appearances life seemed to have returned to normal. Maybe Marissa had decided to pack more of her stuff for the trip to New York. Maybe she'd run into Decco at the flat and stayed on for a bit to ensure he wouldn't be suspicious.

The estate was a ghost town. None of the usual Saturday evening activity. Everyone must have been scared indoors. Nial felt paranoid being the only one walking. If he were to encounter a police patrol they would surely pull him in for questioning. When he got within eyesight of Marissa's house, he paused for a moment to observe from a distance. There was no sign of life anywhere. He could feel the eyes of the neighbors on him from behind laced curtains so he braced himself and walked up to her door with as much confidence as he could muster, and gave the door a sharp tap with his knuckles.

The door opened almost immediately, and there was Marissa, she held the door open just enough for him to enter.

"I was worried something had happened. I came back…"

"To see me?" Dessie said as he shoved the door closed behind Nial. He wrapped his arm around Marissa's neck and held the barrel of a gun to her head just behind her right ear. "Or did you come back to see Marissa?" Dessie grinned as he let his left arm drop and grabbed Marissa's breast roughly. Nial made an instinctive step forward.

"Ah ah ah… easy now, Pat. Or should I call you Nial?" Dessie kept a firm grip on Marissa's breast. He was greasier than ever. A trickle of saliva was running out of the corner of his mouth. He flicked his tongue out to lick it away. "Let's all go inside and take a seat so we can have a little chat, shall we."

Nial looked directly into Marissa's eyes. She looked defeated. He looked away; he didn't want to think about what she might have already endured over the past couple of hours.

"If you hurt her I'll kill you," Nial spat.

"What do you think this is kid, a fucken movie? I'll do the talking and you'll listen up or I'll blow a fucken hole in the side of her head." Dessie sent a spray of spit at Nial. A single tear ran down the side of Marissa's face. Nial turned and walked down the hallway into the living room.

In the corner of the room, Decco was tied to a wooden chair. He had a blindfold over his eyes. From what Nial could see of his face, he could tell it had taken a beating to get him there. Dried blood caked his chin. But he appeared to be still breathing.

Two other men were in the room. One on the couch. Another in a chair by the open window. Both were holding revolvers. One had bright red curly hair and freckles. He was wearing a pea green suit with wide lapels like some 1970s leprechaun pimp.

The other was bald on top. Bell-bottomed brown corduroy trousers and a wrinkled white shirt, stained with what he hoped was Decco's blood. Neither of them spoke.

Dessie shoved Marissa onto the couch next to Freckles. Freckles grinned at Nial.

"What's with the fancy costumes?" Nial said. "You boys with the circus?"

Freckles came off the couch, and without a moment's warning busted Nial's nose with a headbutt. Nial dropped to his knees and cupped his face. He was bleeding. He could feel the metallic drip in the back of his throat. He was stunned. It had happened so quickly.

"Just listen to them Nial," Marissa sobbed.

"You done being a smart-ass?" Dessie said calmly.

Nial nodded.

"Eamon, get up and get the lad a wet towel," Dessie said. "From here on in, just listen like a good cub."

Bell-bottoms got up without a word of complaint and did what he was told. He came back and handed Nial a wet tea towel. Nial held it to his face.

"You have any idea the trouble you're in?" Dessie asked, as he pulled a chair into the center of the room and sat in front of Nial, who was still on his knees. "Thanks to you, your little junkie pal is dead, and two English cops are maimed." Nial was relieved to hear the cops were still alive. He was ready to cling to any raft in this shitstorm. "And now it looks like they're trying to pin the whole thing on the Provos. That's bad for you Nial. Very, very bad indeed."

"I didn't mean—"

"Of course you didn't... you were just trying to kill the man who murdered your brother. I get it, Nial... big fucken hero. Well, ya fucked that up, ya little bollox." Dessie slapped Nial on the side of the head and paused to light a smoke. "You played your hand, and you lost. Am I right?"

Nial nodded.

"Right. So, you wanna hear plan B?"

"What's plan B?"

"Plan B is you're gonna kill somebody else."

"Who?"

Dessie slapped Nial again.

"What did I tell you about asking stupid questions?" Dessie got up and walked over to Marissa. He pushed a strand of hair off her cheek with the barrel of the gun. "If you do what I tell you to do, I'll let this one and that other clown go free."

Decco mumbled something that sounded like a plea for help from under his mask. Marissa looked to Nial for some indication that he was taking this as seriously as he should.

"You promise to let them go?"

"Tell you what, you do what I tell you, and then we'll talk about it... but it'll be hard for me to keep the lads off this one for very long." Freckles grinned a lecherous tar-stained grin at Marissa.

"I'll do it. Only if you promise not to touch her... or

CHURCH END

let these two near her."

"Good man, Nial, you're some cub… you'll go a long way in this business."

"I don't want your business."

"Looks like you're in my business. Come on. Me and you's gonna take a wee drive."

"Where?" Nial asked. Dessie slapped him again, hard, and Nial decided to stop asking questions.

"Nobody touches the girl til I get back?" Dessie said, eyeing his two soldiers. "Do I make myself clear?"

The two men nodded reluctantly.

"This wee bollox doesn't behave himself then you can go to town on her."

The two men smiled and nodded excitedly.

"Not a finger til I get back." Dessie gave Nial a shove toward the door.

Nial took a last glance around the room: Decco mumbling, bound and gagged in a chair. Marissa on the couch with her arms protectively wrapped across her chest. Baldy, in bellbottoms, in a chair by the window. And Freckles, leering at Marissa as if he were poised to molest her the moment Dessie and Nial left the room. "Don't you fucken touch her…" Nial yelled. Freckles gave him a wink as he licked his filthy lips. Dessie shoved Nial on out of the living room into the front hall.

Chapter 22

Outside, the sky was the color of a bad bruise. A heavy jumble of mismatched clouds seemed to be wrestling their way across the evening sky. It was the kind of evening that demanded either a soft bed or a high-stool. Nial walked ahead of Dessie to the Mercedes. The car was parked no more than a hundred yards from Marissa's front door. How had he missed it? He needed to be a smarter criminal if he were to find a way out of this mess. If only he'd been more careful. If only he'd never met The Baz. If only he'd stayed at home in Tyrone and left well enough alone.

As they pulled out of the estate they passed two police officers on foot. They were chatting so intently neither one of them gave the Mercedes a second glance. Nial considered leaping from the car and begging them for help. But before he could take into consideration all the elements at play in such a move, they had moved on. It was best just to roll with it now he decided. No further gamble was worth the loss of Marissa's life.

Nial had been so singularly focused in his rage toward Anderson for so long he'd become blinded to the murderous consequences of stepping so far off the spiritual beam. He could hear his mother's voice, "Are you going to mass every Sunday?" He'd even lied about that. He should have gone to mass. Or at least prayed. He could have gone to work. Become a great carpenter. Sent money home to help his family. He could have been in a hotel in a seaside town right now with Marissa listening to seagulls and the soft roll of the ocean beneath their window.

"Where are you staying?" Dessie asked. He had stopped at a red light about to turn onto Church Road. "Left or right?"

"Left."

The light changed. Dessie turned left toward The White Horse.

"Where?"

"Wilsden."

"You didn't get very far. Where you staying up there?"

"A bed and breakfast."

"Ah… couldn't keep your pecker in your pants long enough to get out of London. Don't blame you. She's some piece of ass that one, eh!"

Nial let it go. He didn't feel like another slap in the mouth.

"She's a chancy wee thing in the sack I bet."

Dessie was baiting him. Nothing to be done. Nial bit his tongue and let it go. Now was not the time.

Dessie sensing that Nial couldn't be baited reached for the radio and turned it to the five o'clock news.

"... Detectives have revealed this afternoon that the terrorist suspect killed in yesterday's bombing in North London was in fact Barry Callaghan, a known IRA expert, believed at this point to be the mastermind behind at least three other bombings in the city over the past two years."

"What!" Nial blurted. "That's bullshit."

Dessie shushed him and turned the radio up another notch or two.

"In a statement released by Scotland Yard, it has been revealed that twenty-two-year-old Callaghan had been hiding out in a derelict flat in the Harlesden Housing Estate, Church End, for some time. A search of the premises provided traces of explosives and clues as to Callaghan's intended targets. Detectives have also recovered a handgun which forensics have linked to the murder of Sergeant Dominic Wilson at his home in Battersea in November of last year. The two detectives who were caught in the blast, Jason Banks and Nigel Dobson, remain in critical condition at this time at The Royal London Hospital. Banks, a fifteen-year veteran on the force, lost an eye in the explosion. Dobson, a father of four young children, is on a ventilator at this time. Speaking from 10 Downing Street this afternoon the prime minister denounced the attack..." There was a brief pause and then the voice of the Margaret Thatcher: "I am quite sure this cowardly terrorist did not act alone. To his accomplices, I say, be warned: there will be no tolerance for brutality and violence on our security forces. We are coming for you. We will find you. And we will punish you."

Dessie roared with delight. "By Jasus you got them boy."

Nial was not nearly as thrilled at his newfound celebrity. He was well aware of Thatcher's "Shoot to Kill" brand of justice back in Tyrone. A British soldier didn't need a court of law to exact justice in Northern Ireland. The unspoken rule in the six counties was that if the British couldn't find enough evidence to convict a suspect… or, if they just wanted rid of someone… they could just shoot them and walk away scot-free. The British had been the greatest military force on the planet, and they didn't like that they were being outsmarted in Northern Ireland by a handful of farmers. Shoot to Kill was a military response to their humiliation on the world stage. Nial knew that news of the police officers wounded in the bombing would most likely result in some innocent lad in Northern Ireland with a bullet in the back of his head. Just like what had happened with his brother. A dark butterfly had flapped its wings.

"By God you showed them. Did you hear that? Thatcher herself on the news! Fuck me, you're a natural, cub."

Nial stared off out the window at the pedestrians. He wanted no part of Dessie's celebrations. There had been no mention of Barry's family back in Dublin. They would be handed a box of body parts to bury. They would spend the rest of their lives wondering about what was true about their darling son. Barry's only crime had been that he was gay and afraid. He'd fallen in love with Nial and it had cost him his life.

And then there were the two officers. Maimed for life, if they were lucky enough to survive their injuries. Do you really survive a bombing? Or do you go on from there as best you can with what you've got left? Dobson had four young children. The bomb had taken their childhoods too. Shards of this emotional shrapnel would rain down for generations to come. One tiny parcel of explosives had sent a ripple of fear through an entire nation. That's what terrorism is, Nial thought... the ability to instill terror in the hearts of innocents. Those young children would carry the irrational fear of small packages, and Irish people, for the rest of their lives. He had become a terrorist.

Dessie was actually laughing now. His eyes were glistening. He was in a state of ecstasy. He reached over, turned the station to find himself some music and found Frankie Goes to Hollywood. That seemed to speak to him. He fine tuned it and turned it way up and started singing along at the top of his lungs as he slapped out the beat on the steering wheel... "Relax don't do it, when you wanna go to it... Relax don't do it when you wanna come..." He slapped the dashboard, and reached over and slapped Nial's thigh utilizing it, no doubt, as part of his extensive drum set. Nial reflexively punched him as hard as he could in the side of the face. The car swerved wildly, almost careening headfirst into a double decker bus. Horns honked. Tires screeched. A woman screamed. Dessie swerved out of the way at the last second and swung the car down the next side street. In a flash he had pulled over, and he was across the consul and had Nial by the throat. He was on top of him, strangling him. He had Nial's head jammed down so far against the door handle that Nial thought for sure his neck would snap. Dessie had all his weight on top of him now and a vice-like grip on his throat. Nial looked up into Dessie's face and saw the blood-red countenance of a wild animal. *This is how I die. This is how I die.* And then… just as he felt himself passing out, the fingers released, and Dessie flopped back over onto his own seat. Nial sat up and struggled to get his breathing back. Dessie was still slapping him hard on the back of the head as Nial felt his breath return. He was alive. He had survived.

"You stupid little cunt. Don't you ever fucken put your hands on me again. Do you fucken hear me?" His bottom lip was bleeding. Nial had connected. Dessie put the back of his hand to his mouth and seeing the blood, slapped Nial again. "You ever try anything like that again I'll take you back and tie you in a chair next to your buddy put a gag in your mouth and let you watch the lads go to town on your girl for the night. Would you like to see that? Would you?"

"No."

Dessie slapped him one last time. Then he got out of the car. Walked around to the trunk. He took out a small duffle bag. Got back in the car and dropped the duffle bag in Nial's lap. "There's a man I need you to get rid of. Everything you need in the bag. You have twenty-four hours to get the job done or your girlfriend dies… right after me and the lads give her a bit of a workout that is. It's five fifteen right now. Twenty-four hours starts now. Get the fuck out of my car."

"What am I supposed to do?"

"Get out of my car."

"You want me to kill somebody… who? What is this?"

"The clock is ticking." Dessie slipped the handgun from the inside of his jacket and pointed it at Nial. "When you're done, you come back and find me at your girlfriend's' place. We'll be waiting."

"But…"

"Out, or you'll be on the side of the street looking through that duffle bag with a hole in your leg. Out, while you're still ahead."

Nial took the duffle bag and got out. Dessie swung the car out and he was gone.

Nial looked down at the bag he held in his right arm. He tried to gauge its contents by the weight. What did a gun weigh? Was it another bomb?

Whatever else it was, it was also a key. It was a key to another door he wished he didn't have to open.

Chapter 23

Nial had hoped to slip up to his room in the bedsit without running into Roger. He needed a moment to wash up, regroup, sit for a minute just to catch his breath. So much had happened in the past twenty-four hours and now he feared he had backed himself even further into a corner where he was going to have to commit some new crime. The duffle bag dangling at the end of his arm seemed to gain weight with every step he took. Roger stepped out from the dining room just as he reached the top landing.

"Will you care for a drop of tea?"

Nial paused for a moment. He didn't want Roger to catch the pain in his eyes. There was also the possibility of blood on his face from the slapping he'd taken from Dessie.

"No," Nial answered softly without turning. "I think I just need to lay down for a moment. Thank you though."

"I'll make you a pot and leave it outside your door," Roger said in a comforting tone that seemed an answer to Nial's repressed anguish. "I'll just give the door a tap and leave it on the floor out there, and you can take it at your leisure."

"Thanks, Roger."

Once he saw himself in the bathroom mirror he was relieved that he hadn't turned to face Roger. A trickle of dried blood ran from his nose to his upper lip. His cheeks were red, his hair was badly tossed, and he had the imprint of two big hands on his throat.

He left the duffle bag on the bed unopened, undressed, and stepped into the bathtub to wash.

He was toweling off when he heard a light tap on the door and then Roger's soft footsteps retreating back down the stairs. Outside the door he found a silver tray with a steaming pot of tea, a plate of ham, cheese, and tomato sandwiches, cut into neat triangles, and a small saucer of biscuits; Digestives and bourbon creams. He hadn't realized how hungry he was until he saw the pleasant display of food. He took it inside and devoured all of it at once. Every last crumb.

It was almost seven thirty before he opened the duffle bag. He blessed himself and ripped open the zipper. Inside was a brown manila envelope and an explosive device about the size of an encyclopedia. He removed the envelope and carefully set it on the bed. He examined the device. A dark metal box with a switch on top. A piece of red tape in the shape of an arrow pointed to the switch. There was nothing protecting the switch, anything that knocked against it could have set it off.

Nial shuddered at the thought. He carefully opened the manila envelope and slipped out a single slip of paper with a typed note:

Hand deliver the duffle bag to Alan Jarvis.
23 Parkside Ave, Wimbledon
Open the bag. Hit the detonator (the red switch on top) and walk away.
You'll have thirty seconds to get as far away as possible once you hit the switch.

What sort of an idiot built this thing? Maybe he was supposed to hit the switch accidentally. Maybe he was the intended target. Was Dessie clearing up his own mess? Nial discarded the thought. He had an address. He had a bomb. And he was expected to deliver it. He was trading the life of Jarvis for Marissa and Decco... and possibly his own.

It was a crude plan. But maybe that was the reality of this life: it was crude. Crude men. Crude instructions. Crude bombs. Maybe Jarvis was just as crude. Maybe he would come to the door and pick up the duffle bag without a thought.

Anyway, it was too late in the day to attempt to deliver it tonight. Even if he left now he wouldn't be in Wembley before ten o'clock. He would get some sleep and go first thing in the morning.

Could he really drop it on the doorstep tap the door and walk away? What if Jarvis' wife opened the door? Or, God forbid, one of his kids lifted the bag? Who was Jarvis? Why did he deserve to die? Is this how soldiers felt when they were asked to kill in war? Was he capable of murdering a man he felt no personal animosity toward?

Nial cracked open the window overlooking the backyard and lit a smoke. It was dark out. And raining again. In truth, his head was spinning. He had no idea what to do from here. There was no clear path forward. No easy way out. There was another way of life out there, a simpler way, and he was missing out on all of it. He had the strange sense that down below his window just now, Roger's roses had their faces tipped upward, petals spread, embracing every drop of rain they could catch… smiling at the sky.

Chapter 24

Nial woke with a start. For a second he thought he was at home in bed in Tyrone and that his mother was at the door. It took him a moment to realize he was in a bedsit, in London, fully dressed on a bed right next to a bomb. He remembered finishing his cigarette and lying down for a moment on the bed. How much time had passed?

"There's someone here to see you," Roger said.

"What?" Nial said, carefully placing the manila envelope in the bag again.

"A man, said he's here to see you." Roger waited for Nial to respond, but Nial didn't know what to say. No one knew where he was. Had Marissa told them where they were staying? Maybe it was Dessie. Or the cops. No, if it were the cops, Roger would have said so. "Should I send him up?"

"Sure," Nial responded, even though he was not sure at all.

Nial zippered the duffle bag and slipped it under the bed.

There was a knock on the door. He braced himself and opened it.

To his astonishment, there stood his old work mate, John The Burner.

The Burner regarded Nial with a smile.

"Soft day."

Nial had nothing to say. He stepped aside and let The Burner enter the room.

"Ah now... would ye look at this... lovely wee room? Roger seems like a decent sort..."

"What are you doing here?" Nial said after he'd closed the door.

"Thought I'd drop up to see you."

"How did you know where to find me?"

"What do they charge for a place like this?"

"John... what the fuck are you doing here?"

"Reminds me of a little place I stayed years back in Germany," The Burner said settling into a spot on the bed, placing a couple of cushions behind his back for comfort. "There was a girl, Hilda... or was it Hannah..."

"John, what are you doing in my room?"

"Oh, right... of course... well, it's a long story."

"I have a few minutes."

"Well do you remember yer man who saw you drop the bag of cement on Harry?"

"Yes."

"Well he squealed on you."

"What? That fucker."

"No good deed goes unpunished. You've got to

watch out for your own in this town. Harry offered him a job as a ganger if he gave up a name and he gave them yours… Pat."

"Bastard."

"Cops came sniffing around after you left work Friday, so I took it upon myself to come and give you a heads-up. I knew you lived in Church End Estate, but I hadn't a clue where to start looking in there so went to The White Horse instead. Figured I'd find you with a nose bag strapped on in there. No luck. Nobody'd ever seen or heard of you in there. A wary bunch, not given to strangers asking questions. Not even that bitter little barman Martin would give you up. Is there some wee thing wrong with that man?"

"Tourette's."

"Ah, so there I was turned for home. Just about to pull out of a parking spot up the street, and lo and behold…?"

"The bomb."

"A bomb. Gave me a bit of a jolt to be honest. Anyhoo… I knew the place would be crawling with cops after that so I high-tailed it on out of Harlesden quick as I could."

"So how did you find me…"

"Well, the whole thing didn't sit right with me, you see… My gut wouldn't let it sit… Couldn't shake the sense that some wee thing was awry. So I turn on the morning news and I'm hearing news of this lad Barry Callaghan, and he sounded a bit like that might have been the lad you shared a flat with, Baz, am I right?"

Nial nodded.

"Sorry for your loss," The Burner offered sincerely.

"Thank you."

"So, says I to meself, maybe the lad's in a spot of bother. I'll take a spin up north again and I'm pulling into Church End Estate and what I do see?" Nial shakes his head. "A black Mercedes Benz, and the bold Dessie Doyle behind the wheel and two colorful-looking goons in the car with him. Now, says I to meself, that's strange. What would Dessie want in this estate, the morning after a bomb? Not that what he does is any business of mine mind you... what a man does is..."

"So..."

"So, I followed him. And I watch himself and these two circus clowns he's with enter one of the flats in there. And then just a little while later a pretty girl shows up..."

"Marissa."

"Is that her name? Marissa. Lovely looking girl altogether. And she goes into the same flat. So I wait. And I wait. Because something about it doesn't feel right. And guess who shows up next?"

"Me."

"Yourself. Correct."

"So you followed me back here when Dessie after dropped me off?"

"Thought for sure you were done for when he swerved for the bus. Thought I was going to have to step in when he was choking you..."

"I had it under control."

"Never doubted it for a second. So then I had to have a wee chat with meself... John, says I, do you really need to get involved here? Is this really something you want to stick your big nose into the middle of? And after a while back and forth arguing the ins and outs, I says to meself, says I, sure why not… might as well see if the cub needs some help. So here I am… with my big nose in it."

Nial sighed deeply. It was good to see The Burner. Maybe there was a way out of this yet without anyone else getting killed. "I'm in some deep shit."

"It would appear that way."

"I don't know what to do."

The Burner leaned back, and knitting his hands behind his head, said, "How about you tell me your side of the story first and we'll take it from there?"

"Okay."

"Nay panic," The Burner said in his slow drawl, closing his eyes to settle in for the story.

"If there's to be panic, let it be organized," Nial said. The Burner opened one eye and smiled at him.

Nial told The Burner the whole story, from Cathal's death, right through to the duffle bag under the bed. The Burner kept his eyes closed the entire time, and were it not for the occasional moan, or nod of the head, Nial would have assumed he was asleep for the whole thing.

When he was sure Nial was finished, he spoke without opening his eyes.

"And this duffle bag, with the bomb… is under the bed I'm sitting on?"

"Yes."

"Aha. Can I take a look at it?"

Nial pulled the bag from under the bed and handed

it to The Burner. The Burner opened the bag and examined the note and the bomb. "So you just hit this switch, then you have thirty seconds to drop the bag, knock the door, and get away?"

"That's what the note says."

"Isn't that ingenious! I wonder what sort of explosives they use for a thing like this."

"I don't think it matters."

"Maybe plastic? Or would it be dynamite?"

"John… I don't know how they build bombs. That's not really my concern right now."

"Mmmm. And he wants you to deliver it to Jarvis?"

"Yes."

"Well, that's interesting."

"Why is that interesting?"

"Alan Jarvis owns a labor company… Jarvis Labor… McGinley's main labor competitor at the Kings Cross library job… and many other big jobs around town I assume."

"Why would the IRA want Jarvis dead?"

"My guess is, they wouldn't."

"But Dessie sold me a bomb to get rid of Anderson."

"The IRA don't sell bombs, Pat… excuse me, Nial… That's going to take some getting used to… You look like a Pat."

"So Dessie's not in the IRA!"

"Dessie's a bollox. He gets you a bomb knowing it will be pinned on the Provos. Then he gets rid of Jarvis with another bomb, and then he kills you, and anybody else who could give him up, and he eliminates his labor competition. I'd imagine that's worth an awful lot of money to a man like Dessie."

"He's doing it for the money?"

"You sound surprised."

"Marissa."

"First thing we need to do is get you out of here in case he shows up. You can come stay at my place til we come up with a plan."

"We need to go now… what if he…"

"Once step at a time. Let's get out of here first."

Nial grabbed a few items of clothing and threw them in Marissa's bag while The Burner lifted the duffle bag off the bed.

"I'll handle this from here if you don't mind."

On their way out, Nial stopped to settle up with Roger. He was sitting alone in the small kitchen in back, having tea, listening to classical music on a small transistor radio.

Roger didn't ask any questions about why he was leaving, or who the mysterious visitor had been, but Nial sensed he understood more about his situation than he cared to say. Roger was better than all that.

With great care, Roger singled out a rose from a vase on the table and handed it to Nial.

"Give this to your girl when you see her." Roger looked away as Nial took the rose and Nial followed his eyes to a framed picture on the wall next to the door. It was a younger Roger, on a beach towel next to pretty girl. She was smiling. Pearls of sea water glistened on her bare shoulders. Nial didn't need Roger to tell him she was gone.

"She'll like this," Nial said. "Thank you."

Outside, the street was glazed in the aftermath of a fresh shower. He followed The Burner up the street to a light blue Mark 11 Ford Escort with Republic of Ireland license plates.

"You drove this all the way from Galway?"

"Saoirse."

"Seer who?

"Her name is Saoirse... Irish for Freedom." The Burner said tapping the roof with his hand. "She hasn't let me down yet."

Chapter 25

The Burner's spacious bedsit in Hammersmith was immaculate. The bedcovers were folded down tight as a drum. Military style. A television against one wall was flanked floor to ceiling with packed bookshelves. The walls were adorned with old art, oil canvases in antique frames. Black-and-white photographs professionally framed and matted. A collection of antique wood planes sat on a shelf above the sink. A lamp in the corner bathed the room in a soft orange glow. This was not your typical Paddy pad in London. But there had never been anything typical about The Burner.

"Tae?" The Burner asked, lifting a kettle to fill it under the tap.

"Tae? I thought you had a plan. Shouldn't we be doing something?"

"Nay panic. Nay panic. We're not going to go rushing in there like a couple of bulls in a china shop. We'll have the tae."

"For fuck's sake, John. We can't leave her up there all night."

"We'll have the tae."

"That's your plan? Have Tae?"

"That's the only part I've come up with so far."

"I can't just leave her there."

"We won't… but I need to have the tae… and I need to think."

Nial had no intention of relaxing. The thought of Marissa spending the night under the same roof as those degenerate thugs sickened him. But The Burner was not to be rushed, and right now The Burner was the only hope Nial had left. He needed to be patient. Trust that The Burner had his ways. Let him think.

Nial walked over and ran his finger across the book spines. Most were Irish themed. Books on history, politics, myth, and poetry. Nial plucked one out and took a seat on a dark blue antique velvet couch.

"Is it okay to sit on this thing?"

"It's survived this long. I'm sure it'll survive you too. Sugar?"

"You have any beer?"

"Sugar?"

"Two. Is this one any good?" Nial said, holding up a random book he'd chosen: *The Great Hunger,* by Cecil Woodham-Smith.

"It's a start in the right direction," The Burner said, carefully ladling two spoons of sugar into a mug. "What do you know of history?"

"Just what they taught us in school: Churchill, Clement Attlee, Harold McMillan…"

"Not English history you clown... Your own history."

"Oh, Neville Chamberlain?"

"What about Wolfe Tone?" The Burner asked turning to face him. Nial shook his head. "Daniel O'Connell? Padraig Pearse? James Connolly? Surely you've heard of Thomas Clarke?"

Nial shook his head.

"Thomas Clarke?" The Burner repeated. Nial continued to shake his head. "First name on the Proclamation... A Tyrone man, like yerself. You never heard his name?"

"Don't think so."

"By God they done some job robbing you lads of your heritage up there. My, my, my. That's the heartbreak of colonization right there: forcing the oppressor's version of history on the children. They never taught you about The Famine or The Rising?"

"I think I heard something about The Famine... it was to do with the potatoes, right?"

The Burner shook his head and turned back to the kettle. "No greater crime than to wipe out a man's heritage... Take away all that explains to them who they are or where they came from. It's a mortal sin... slaughter of the soul, a crime against humanity."

"... the population was halved." Nial read aloud out of the book but The Burner wasn't listening.

"Promise me something... when all this is over, you survive this thing... you'll go back and read."

"Okay."

"Promise me," The Burner snapped, spinning around. "Or by Jasus I'll throw you into the street right now and you can go out and figure this thing out by yourself."

Nial had never seen him so fired up.

"Okay."

"And if you have children, teach your children."

"I will. I promise."

"Right then," The Burner said, settling himself again with a deep sigh, regaining his composure. "We'll have the tae. You can't bate the cup of tae."

"You can't bate it."

"You cannot," The Burner said, handing Nial a steaming mug of tea and settling into a comfy armchair in the corner.

"Barry's?" Nial asked, taking a sip.

"Tetley."

"Tetley? I wouldn't have took you for a Tetley tea man."

"The Tetley's yer only man."

"Really?"

"Tetley is a far superior tea. Barry's has the brand recognition, I'll give you that, and, I would argue, a hint of Republicanism about it… but the name's misleading. It's not Irish at all, there is no real Irish tea. Barry's is African tea. Too harsh for me."

"You sure it's not made in Dublin…"

"Dublin me hole… Where would you grow tea in Ireland? You need sun, man."

"So Tetley is not grown in England?"

"Tetley might have a trace of colonialism about it alright… Definitely got some blood on it's hands…"

"Blood?" Nial said, frowning into his cup of tea.

"… But not, in my humble opinion, nearly so

bloody as say, your cup of Punjab."

"No Punjab."

"Punjab has the bitter taste of the empire about it," The Burner continued. He'd given this some thought.

"And Tetley doesn't?"

"Can you taste any hint of British colonialism in that cup of tea?"

Nial took another sip as The Burner watched him intently.

"Not a bit." Though in truth, he hadn't a clue if that was even a thing. What would colonialism taste like?

"See," The Burner said, with a self-satisfied grin. "That's what I'm telling you."

Nial understood that this was a ridiculous conversation, but he knew from the time he'd spent working with The Burner that the man took his cup of tea very, very seriously.

"The Tetley's yer only man," The Burner concluded.

"It's a grand cup of tae. Thank you," Nial said, delighted to see the discussion come to some sort of conclusion so he could circle it back to the matter at hand. Nial took another sip before making the shift.

"Maybe I should turn myself in to the cops."

"Are ye mad?"

"Maybe we might have a better chance of getting Marissa and Decco out of there unharmed."

"First sniff of a cop around that squat and Dessie'll waste her and come out guns blazing ... or he'll use her as a hostage to make his escape. Then you'll go off to prison for the rest of your life, and, God forbid, me, as your accomplice. No. Absolutely not. No cops."

"So we have to get them out."

"We have to get them out."

"How?"

"There might be somebody we could ask for help."

"Who?"

"The lads." The Burner said, giving Nial a sly wink. Nial had no idea what he was talking about.

"What lads?"

"The lads. The Provos. The IRA."

"The RA?"

"I can't imagine they're real happy about this current publicity. My guess is they'd like to get their hands on that duffle bag we have in the back of the car before you go dropping it off in Wembley causing more trouble for them. They already have Thatcher on the news giving her boys in the army itchy fingers back in the North over this whole thing. Dessie's making them look bad... putting their men in danger. Maybe we let them know where they can get their hands on him."

"Dessie?"

"They might want to help out."

"What are the chances they'll get Marissa out safely?"

"I've no idea, but they're our best shot. I doubt the police would be worried about a few Irish squatters getting caught in the crossfire as long as they get their man."

"And what about me? I was the one who started all this. The Provos are not going to happy with me. I could get kneecapped, or worse."

"There's a good possibility of that alright," The

CHURCH END

Burner said, getting up and getting the teapot. "Wee hot drop?"

"Sure," Nial said, holding his cup out for The Burner to top it off. "So you think I could get kneecapped?"

"It's possible. It's possible. We have a little leverage though we might be able to use in our favor."

"What's that?"

"Me. I know everything. I can tell them that if they touch you, I go to the cops. I could tell them if anything happens to either one of us, I have evidence in a secure location and the cops will have all of it."

"Will that work?"

"Haven't a clue."

"How do we find the Provos?"

"The phone book."

"They're listed in the phone book?"

"No, they're not listed in the phone book. I have a friend that I could go see."

"Can we go now?"

"You'll have to stay here," The Burner said, opening the door of a small closet and removing a finely tailored long black coat and a dark gray gambler's hat. With his black boots, he looked like a character out of an old western movie. "Don't answer the door to anyone. I don't get guests, ever. I have my own key so I won't be knocking. If someone knocks on that door, go out the bathroom window; there's a flat roof there that will lead you to an alleyway in back."

"You've thought about all this?"

"Do not go out while I'm gone. Do not open this door. You hear me? Get some sleep. There's food in the fridge, help yourself. I'll be back when I can."

After The Burner left the flat, Nial stretched out on the couch and closed his eyes. His head was swimming with everything that had happened in the last couple of days. He'd lost all sense of time since he'd picked up that bomb in Leicester Square. When was that? Friday? Two days ago. That meant this was Sunday night. He'd missed mass again. Maybe it was all a bad dream. Maybe if he could fall sleep and wake up everything would be back to normal.

Chapter 26

It was just after midnight by the time The Burner returned. Nial had not slept. The Burner was not alone. Another man followed him through the door.

"This is Brendan," The Burner said, closing the door behind them. "Brendan, Nial."

The Burner went on to the sink to fill the kettle. More tae.

Brendan and Nial were left to face each other. Brendan shook a cigarette out of a pack. Nial eyed them hungrily. He'd smoked his last a couple of hours back and didn't feel safe going out for a fresh pack. Brendan held the pack toward Nial. Nial took one and Brendan lit them both.

"Everybody for tae?" The Burner asked, putting the kettle on the stove. No one was expected to answer, and they didn't… of course everyone was having tea.

Brendan was a much bigger man than John. He had a round barrel chest and a pair of dark brooding eyes that seemed to hide in the shadow of his thick brows. He moved to The Burner's armchair and let himself down with a sigh.

"Well, what's the story with this Dessie bastard?"

Nial glanced at The Burner. The Burner gave him a look that said, *Tell the man what he wants to know.*

Nial took a seat on the blue couch. "He's got my girl and another lad in a flat in Harlesden."

"Who's this other lad?"

"Decco. A biker... a lad that shares the flat with Marissa. He was tied to a chair last time I saw him."

"And what about these other clowns?"

"I dunno know. They looked dangerous to me."

"Dangerous or stupid?"

"Both."

"Any guns on them?"

"Dessie has a gun. Not sure about the other two. I didn't see any."

"What's this I hear about you gonna blow up some man in a repair shop?"

"Anderson... he shot my brother."

"And you come over here with your dick in your hand—"

"He killed my brother."

"Shhh..." Brendan said, sitting forward, putting his finger to his lips. "You come over here, with your dick in your hand like you're John Wayne... and now we have a huge fucken mess on our hands." Brendan didn't raise his voice, but Nial could feel the power of the man from across the room. He could see his chest move up and down in measured breaths like he was holding back the sea. "Do you know who I am?"

Nial shook his head.

"I'm the only Irishman in this town who decides who lives and who dies. If I don't say it, it doesn't happen. That's how things get done around here. This is my fucken town. My fucken town." Brendan sat forward to make sure he had Nial's full attention. "The only reason my hands are not around your throat right now is because this man spoke for you."

"How many sugars, Brendan?"

"Three."

"It's a big spoon…" The Burner said by way of warning as he turned to show Brendan the evidence. "…for a small spoon. You still want the three?"

"Two will do."

"Cow?"

"Small drop, John, thanks."

Burner sugared and milked the teas and brought them to the two men. The tea absorbed some of the violent energy in the room, the way tea does.

"Lovely drop of tae, John," Brendan said, taking a sip out of the steaming cup.

"Tis indeed. Thanks, John," Nial said. Relieved to have the energy shifted.

"So, we have a problem here…" Brendan began in a more settled tone. "A wee problem to be solved. Couple of tough guys to be taken care of. Bundle of fucken half-wits to be sorted out. Is that what we have… a bunch of fucken half-wits?"

Nial decided not to bother with an answer. Brendan was just working his way through the thing now.

"Right... young fella, give me the spread of the place again. How many in that room? Where exactly was everybody when you last saw them? Best you can."

"Well, there was Dessie, he was on his feet, just sort of walking around... Living room is at the front of the flat, street level. One of the goons was sitting at a table right by the front window. He had the window open a crack next to him far as I remember. The other boy was on the couch next to Marissa, and Decco was tied to a wooden chair."

"And where's that chair?"

"In the corner. Close to the kitchen table. Front of the room."

"Is there a back door to the flat?"

"Not that I know of. Kitchen window is over a small garden area in back though."

"Mmmm. And this Dessie fucker... he's the McGinley's man. Am I right?"

"Right."

"He can handle himself?"

"Yes. He's dangerous."

Brendan smiled at that.

"I'll show him fucken dangerous." Brendan drew deeply on his smoke. "And who am I?"

"You're... Brendan..." Nial offered with some hesitancy.

"No, motherfucker, I am nobody... you never met me... I never existed. You understand?"

"Sorry, yes. Nobody," Nial said giving him the thumbs up.

Brendan stood. Drained the last of his tea.

"Thanks, John."

"You off?"

"I'm gonna go up there and take care of this wee situation."

"I'll go with you," Nial said, standing.

"The fuck you will," Brendan growled. "I'll take care of this myself."

"You can't. There's too many of them…"

"Back it up, cub," Brendan said, stepping up to Nial.

"I'm coming."

"I'm just about fucken done with you and your fucking family," Brendan snapped.

"What?" Nial said. Maybe he'd misheard. Brendan continued to glower down at him, his lower jaw grinding back and forth like he was trying to knock his molars out of place. Nial got the sense that Brendan had said more than he'd intended to. "What do you mean: 'my fucking family'?"

"Men… let's be …" The Burner started, but Nial cut him off.

"No. What do you mean: 'my family'?"

"Your brother was a scumbag," Brendan said coldly.

Nial swung for Brendan but Brendan caught his fist in his big meaty hand and clamped down on it like a vice until Nial thought his bones would turn to dust.

"Brendan. I took you here in good faith," The Burner said softly, but Brendan never so much as glanced in his direction.

"Your brother was a smart-ass… couldn't keep his fucken mouth shut. Put men's lives in danger. Good men. If Anderson hadn't put one in the back of his head, we'd have done it ourselves. He got what he deserved."

"Cathal wasn't in the fucken IRA, he'd never hurt a fly."

Brendan snorted a disdainful laugh.

"You didn't know your brother very well, son."

"I'm not your fucking son."

"John," Brendan said, shoving Nial at him like he was a rag doll. "Keep this wee fucker out of my way. I'm goin' to clean up this fucken mess. I ever see or hear from you again, kid, I'll bury you with your brother."

Brendan turned, opened the door, and he was gone.

"He'll get them all killed," Nial said as soon as he was sure Brendan was out the door.

"Best let it be now," said John.

"No."

"It's the way it has to be."

Nial eyed a gleaming butcher knife in a holder by the sink. He dashed over, grabbed it, and before The Burner could stop him, Nial was in the bathroom, the door bolted behind him. He pulled open the window, dropped onto the flat roof, into the back alley, and he was gone.

Chapter 27

When he reached Harlesden, Nial had the taxi pull up on the dual carriageway across from Church End Estate. He paid the driver and ran in the direction of Marissa's flat. It had been foolish not to go directly to the cops. Brendan was going to kill everyone in that flat to get to Dessie. He was a monster. Marissa didn't stand a chance.

From the front of the house, nothing seemed amiss. Dessie's black Mercedes was still sitting in the parking lot exactly where it had been before. The curtains were drawn over the lighted living room window. The window was slightly ajar. It was just after midnight. Hopefully they weren't all awake inside. Nial decided to circle around to the back to see if perhaps he might be able to creep in through the kitchen window. He didn't have a plan. He was just moving on instinct.

Most of the windows in the estate were in darkness. There wasn't a single person out and about. Nial cleared the small brick wall into the grassy area behind the squat hoping not to land on broken glass. There were no working streetlights back there, so it was hard to see where he was going.

A dog in a neighboring yard rattled a heavy chain and began barking ferociously. Nial hit the ground and lay face down in the long grass. The yard was unkempt. The grass was at least knee deep back there and provided fair coverage. A light appeared in the kitchen window of Marissa's squat. Nial tipped his head toward the window to watch the shadow of a figure approach the window. The curtain was pulled back in the corner. It was Dessie. Brendan was not there yet.

Dessie pressed his face to the glass peering in the direction of the barking dog next door. He'd been spooked. He'd be on alert now. Nial had no idea what to do from here. He'd gone into this blindly. Maybe there was nothing he could do to save Marissa. But he had to believe he'd tried. He had to try.

A window opened on the neighboring house and the voice of an English man yelled at the dog, "'Ere… cut it out. Rex. Lie down ya bloody fool. Rex. Shhh." The dog gave an unhappy growl and the barking stopped.

The neighbor's window closed, and Nial watched Dessie slowly slide open the kitchen window so he could get his head out to peer around. He was not convinced the danger had passed. Nial stayed stock-still and held his breath. Dessie was no more than a few feet away, but the light in the kitchen was bright and Dessie was straining to see anything outside in the dark. Nial clenched the handle of the knife in his right hand and braced himself for an attack. This might be his only chance. If he was fast enough, he could bury the knife in Dessie's throat before he could get his head back in the window. He poised himself to spring. One... Two... Something inside the squat distracted Dessie, and he hurriedly pulled his head back inside again letting the curtain fall.

Nial lifted his head to see Dessie's shadow move a couple of feet away from the open window. What could have distracted him? Was Brendan there already... at the front door?

He crawled quickly through the long grass until he was directly under the window. Rex was at the end of his chain again, barking like crazy. Nial raised himself and gingerly pushed back the corner of the curtain. Dessie was facing away toward the kitchen door. He had the gun in his right hand pointed down the hallway toward the front door of the squat. He had Marissa braced tightly against him as a shield under his left arm.

There were two muffled gunshots inside toward the front of the flat.

"Sean. Eamon," Dessie yelled. "Sean. What's happening out there?"

Brendan must have come through the front window into the house. Neither Sean nor Eamon called back. The clowns were dead. Dessie was on his own now.

Dessie pulled Marissa tight in front of him and put the barrel of the gun to her head. He was too far away from the window. There was no way Nial could get inside fast enough to get to him without him putting a bullet in Marissa's head.

Brendan appeared in the kitchen door with his gun trained on Dessie. Nial dropped away from the window for fear Brendan, put one in his head too. "I take it you're Dessie," he heard Brendan say.

"Don't move or she gets it," Dessie replied.

"Let her go," Brendan said calmly. "She has nothing to do with this."

"Okay, okay… easy…" Dessie pleaded. "We can work this out. I'll put my gun down, and…."

There was one shot. Nial heard a heavy thud as a large body hit the floor. And then footsteps running out of the kitchen. He jumped up and pulled back the curtain to see Marissa slide down the kitchen cabinets until she was seated on the floor, sobbing. Brendan was slumped against the wall by the kitchen door, with a trickle of blood running from a small round hole in the middle of his forehead. His eyes wide in disbelief. Dessie had beaten him to the punch. Dessie reappeared down the hallway from the living room and ran for the front door. Then he stopped and turned to see Nial. He raised the gun. He had a clear shot to take Nial out. Nial braced himself for the shot, but Dessie seemed to decide against it. He lowered the gun. Dessie turned, then he was gone, out the front door, into the night.

Nial put his hand on Marissa's shoulder and she jumped.

"Wait here," he said as he moved past her quickly, grabbed Brendan's gun from his hand, and ran into the living room. The goons were dead. Slumped where they had been sitting. He moved to Decco, but he was dead also. Nial lifted Decco's head. His eyes were wide and wild. It appeared at a glance as if he'd suffocated on the gag.

Nial ran for the front door and out into the night

with the gun raised, but Dessie was already peeling out of the parking lot in the Mercedes. Nial lowered the gun. It was over.

Nial heard the first siren in the distance. He needed to get Marissa out of there as quickly as possible. He turned to go back inside but was startled by the figure of a man stepping out from behind a tree. He instinctively leveled the gun in the man's direction.

"Easy there… easy there," came The Burner's slow drawl.

"John, what are you doing here?"

"Figured you might need some help."

"Brendan's dead, Decco's dead… the other two…"

"The girl?"

"She's okay."

"Good."

"Dessie got away."

"Did he now?" The Burner said, holding up the duffle bag. He turned it upside down and gave it a shake. It was empty.

"What did you do with it?"

"I dunno. Maybe it dropped out under the driver's seat of Dessie's car." There was an enormous explosion somewhere off in the direction of Church Road. "Oops. That must have been it."

A ball of flames could be seen over the tops of the flats.

"Best get that wee girl sorted. That'll hold the cops off for a minute but we best hightail it out of here."

Nial dashed back into the flat. Marissa was where he had left her in the kitchen.

"We have to run."

"What about Decco?"

Nial shook his head. "We need to move. The cops are on their way. You have to get your passport. Get it… anything else you need, quickly. We have to go."

Marissa seemed to snap out of it. She sprang to her feet and bounded up the stairs.

The Burner stepped into the living room and examined Decco.

"This your biker friend?"

Nial nodded.

"Poor bastard." The Burner leaned over and whispered the act of contrition into his ear. By the time he was done, Marissa was back down the stairs and the sound of sirens had gotten frightfully close.

"We right?" The Burner said, dashing out the door, leading them both.

"We're right," Nial said.

They followed The Burner across the parking lot and into a dark alleyway directly across from the flat just as two squad cars, sirens wailing, roared up to the front of the flat. The Burner slowed to a steady walk.

"Nay panic now. Nay panic. We stay calm we're home free."

Nial and Marissa settled into a nice strolling pace alongside The Burner, and he led them to his blue Ford Escort parked at the foot of Church Road.

They stood for a moment and gazed at the hive of emergency vehicles descending on the huge fireball at the upper end of Church Road. Dessie had almost made it out of the north end of the estate when his car had exploded. An army of locals in pajamas, bathrobes, and bedroom slippers were emerging bleary-eyed from their homes to trudge in the direction of the flame, like a platoon of drugged moths.

The Burner opened the driver door and gave the roof a little tap.

"Time to go, children."

"Good to see you, Saoirse." Nial said.

"Saoirse?" Marissa asked.

"Freedom," Nial said. "He named his car Freedom."

Chapter 28

Nial woke to the sound of The Burner putting the kettle on the stove for the tae. He had fallen asleep fully dressed on The Burner's bed. Marissa was asleep in the crook of his arm. The Burner looked over when he stirred.

"I'm going to leave for work in a few minutes," whispered The Burner.

"You're going to work?"

"Best I do what I always do. That way there's no suspicion. They shouldn't have anything connecting me to the scene anyway. But let's play it safe for a few days to be sure."

"What about Brendan... when you picked him up?"

"No one saw me. He lives alone... lived."

Marissa stirred and looked around. She looked up into Nial's face, and she smiled briefly, then she tensed suddenly and frowned.

"Are we safe?"

"We're safe."

"Is it over?"

CHURCH END

"It's over."

"Is it really over?"

"It's over."

The Burner turned the dial on a small radio on a shelf next to the stove.

"News'll be on in a minute. Nothing in the papers yet. Been too late for them to get anything in print."

"You were out already?"

"Went for a bit of a walk to clear my head."

"You must be wrecked."

"There'll be time enough for sleep later. We need to keep the heads clear right now, get you two out of this safely. Shhhh… here it is," he said, turning the dial on the little radio.

"Good morning, this is the BBC. Five people are dead in Harlesden this morning in what police are describing as a drug deal gone bad. The carnage happened in the troubled Church End Estate where, just a few days ago, two police officers were badly hurt in a bomb blast that took the life of an Irish national. Our reporter on the scene spoke briefly to Sergeant William Hayes, in charge of the investigation.

'Can you tell us if this is connected to the bombing here in Church End Estate on Friday?'

'It's too early to say, but it does seem that perhaps there may be some connection.'

'Does this mean that the bombing on Friday might also have been drug related rather than sectarian in nature?'

'We are certainly entertaining that possibility at this

point. What has become clear is that the lawlessness in Church End Estate has reached a fever pitch and that starting today, I am launching a campaign to rid this park, once and for all, of the criminal element that has become entrenched here over the last few years.'

'When you say 'criminal' are you referring specifically to the Irish squatters in the area?'

'They certainly represent quite a swath of the demographic here, yes. Let me just state that the decent, hard-working families of Church End Estate do not deserve to live in fear. Mark my words: the days of the Wild West in Harlesden are over.'

'Do you have any leads at this time into who might be responsible here?'

'It's too early to answer that question, but early indications are that all those responsible for this massacre are dead.'

'Thank you, Sergeant.'

That was our reporter Veronica Dawes in Harlesden. Thank you, Veronica. In other news, both of the police officers who were injured in Friday's blast have been moved from ICU late yesterday evening and are in stable condition. They are expected to survive their injuries...."

The Burner switched off the radio. "Boy, oh boy. Looks like you dodged a bullet on this one," he said. "Someone was looking out for you two along the way."

Nial understood there was much to be grateful for: he was still a free man, he still had his life and limbs, Marissa was alive and safe in his arms, but in his heart, he knew that there was little here to celebrate. He laid

CHURCH END

back in the bed and Marissa rested her head on his chest. He thought of The Baz, Decco, his brother Cathal. Three young lives cut short. Brendan, Dessie, and even the two goons dead in the squat. They had families somewhere too no doubt, praying for their safe return. Two innocent police officers, scarred for life. And after all of this, Anderson had walked free. Unscathed by all of it. Nial had failed. He'd followed a path of rage and revenge and it had torn a ragged path through his soul. There was no walking away from this. There was no freedom. He would carry the scar now always. He imagined the shadow of death would dull the color and taste of everything that would follow, no matter where he went. He had taken a dark path and it had failed to bring the relief he sought. Maybe Cathal had not been the innocent he had imagined him to be. Maybe he too had blood on his hands. Nial made a silent pledge in his heart that from this moment forth, he would move back toward the light. Maybe there was still a way back to some sense of peace of mind, if he focused on giving something back to the world, and those around him. He would attempt to repay the universe for what his selfishness had taken. He was going to go back to church... that would be a start... any church... it didn't fucking matter... What mattered from here on out was that he would be a little kinder in his heart, kinder in the world, more generous in his spirit. Maybe, he thought, when you boiled it all down, when you got to the root of all the historical religious texts, that was all there was... one great universal sacred screed: Don't be a dick. Don't be a fucking dick.

From here on out, he was going to try not to be a

dick. He would pray for the strength to forgive Anderson. He would start there, in his own heart: forgiveness. Let the healing spread from there.

"You can stay here til you're sorted," The Burner said, pouring the steaming water into the teapot. "There's nay panic. Mi casa es su casa."

"Thank you, John," Nial said. "I think we're going to get our passports sorted and go to New York as soon as possible."

"Amerikay," The Burner said. "There you go. That's the stuff. Get out while you can. This town's no place for an Irishman."

"And you'll come visit?" said Marissa.

"I thought you'd never ask." The Burner smiled. "Tae?" he said holding up the pot.

"I'll have a cup," Marissa said, sitting up in the bed.

"I'll have a cup too" added Nial.

"You can't bate the cup of tae," said The Burner.

"You can't bate it," Nial agreed.

"It can't be bate," said Marissa.

Author's Note

If you enjoyed reading this book, please do me a huge favor: make a post about it on social media. Perhaps take a picture of you with your copy. Tag me. Or, tag a few friends. Or you could help by telling some of your friends about the book. You might even leave me a rating or brief review on Amazon. Every little bit helps me get the word out. The best publicity is a satisfied reader.

You can find me on Facebook, Twitter, and Instagram. Or, write me at note at my website to say hello, www.colinbroderick.com.

Thank you.

Acknowledgments

Special thanks to Daria Milas for the incredible cover design. Thank you, Daria.

Also very special thanks to my editor Chris Rhatigan for his insightful guidance.

And to those who helped make this book possible in small and large ways: Stephen Owens, Ellen McShane, Noleen Devlin, Kris Herndon, Angela Mulcahy, Liz Leicht, Jim McVeigh, Jason Doherty, Eddie Patton, Noeleen Deeny, Enda Bloomer, Delores Broderick, Len Engesser, Lynne Sindel, Jan Victoria Scott, Mike Farragher, Carrie-Anne Hunter, Brendan Burke, Maureen Christopher, Eamonn McKay, Paul Loughran, Maura Murphy, Catherine Todd, Noleen Neill, John McCann, Lisa McWeeney, Don Cisternino "Magnifico," Martin McFadden, Josh Brolin, Jon Greenhalgh, Michael Fitzpatrick, Tom McCaffrey, Con McCormack, Lisa Sullivan, Cal Kelly. And lastly, to the entire crew who lived in Church End Estate in the late 80s, wherever you may be.

About the Author

Colin Broderick was born in Birmingham, England and raised in County Tyrone in the North of Ireland. He has published three books: *Orangutan*, *That's That*, and *The Writing Irish of New York*. He has also written and directed two feature movies: *Emerald City*, and *A Bend in the River*. He lives in New Jersey with his wife and three children.

Printed in Great Britain
by Amazon